GREY'S LANDING

GREY'S LANDING

A GREY'S HARBOR STORY

LARK GRIFFING

WIND LARK
PUBLISHING

For my friends and fellow authors, J.C. Wing and Jennifer Sivec. Thanks for helping to create the vision of Grey's Harbor.

GREY'S HARBOR SERIES

GREY'S LANDING
A Grey's Harbor Story
by Lark Griffing

GREY'S HARBOR
A Grey's Harbor Anthology
By Carol Cassada
Lark Griffing
Piper Malone
Jennifer Sivec
J.C. Wing

HOPE ADRIFT
A Grey's Harbor Story
By Lark Griffing

Coming Soon ~

HARBOR TIDES
A Grey's Harbor Story
By Lark Griffing

HARBOR SONG
A Grey's Harbor Story
By J.C. Wing

PERFECT SEAS
A Grey's Harbor Story
By Jennifer Sivec

ISBN-13: 978-0-9988719-7-4

Edited by Wing Family Editing

Cover Design by Wicked Whale Publishing

PROLOGUE

*S*he stood on the rocks that surrounded the lighthouse as the waves crashed around her, laughing at her, pulling her skirt into the swirling dark waters. The sea called out to her as she glanced over her shoulder hoping to see him, but of course he wasn't there. A large wave came and crashed against her, chilling her. This was going to be a cold way to die, she told herself as she waited. She hesitated another second and then tipping forward, she fell into the water . The waves grabbed her, took her, drug her seaward.

It was cold.

Bone chilling cold, and she gasped despite her body's desire to try to save itself. She waited, but it didn't happen. No strong hands reached down into the cold water. No one grasped her hair or her dress to haul her to the surface. He never came. Unlike the books she had feasted on where the heroine was saved.

He never came.

The men ran to the rocks, scanning the ocean where they saw her throw herself in. An elderly gentleman with a grizzled beard barked orders.

"There she is. Haul her out, damn it."

The young men with him did his bidding, catching her by her

waist-length hair and pulling it to bring her body closer to the rocks. The two men reached down and drug the hugely pregnant woman from the waves.

"Is she breathing?" the old man asked in a gruff voice, devoid of emotion.

"Barely."

"Madeline, wake up." He ordered in a voice that dared defiance. He reached down and slapped her face. When she didn't respond, he slapped her again. Hard.

Her eyelids fluttered.

"Who is the father of the babe?" he demanded as the younger men stood by helplessly watching. "Tell me!" he shouted.

"Cooper Grey," she whispered.

Her chest heaved. She choked and drew her last breath.

"Cut the babe from her."

"What? No, Mr. Grey."

"I said cut the babe from her. It's no different from a lamb or a cow. Oh, for heaven's sake."

He crouched to complete the deed himself.

In minutes, he drew from the dead woman a small mewling baby boy.

"He may be a bastard, but he's still a Grey."

1

*M*addy Grey bent her head over her cutting table, scrunching her nose up as she considered the piece of glass. It was exquisite, blues and greens swirled in a soft wave pattern. It was going to be a bitch to cut, especially in the curve she had pictured in her head. She pulled the edge of her lower lip between her teeth as she calmed herself. She imagined the cut and her hand holding the tool just right.

Ssswwtt.

She could tell by the sound without even looking that the cut was good. The wheel had done its job against the glass, scribing the surface and breaking the tension. Now the hard part. She picked up the piece of glass in her hands, ignoring the gloves Tripp always insisted she use. But Tripp was gone. He wouldn't be lecturing her again.

She blinked back the moisture threatening in her eyes, then shook her head, trying to clear it. She had work to do.

Expertly she checked the score, testing it. She could see the cut starting to run along the scratched line in the glass. In her right hand she held the running pliers, in her left she steadied the glass.

Just the right amount of pressure.

Clink.

The cut ran along the score and the one piece of glass became two, with a graceful curve along one edge of both. Maddy set aside the piece she didn't want and critically looked at the other. The curve complemented the wave swirl of colors.

She picked up a clear piece of glass and her large circle cutter. She could do this in her sleep. A quick scribe of the circle and a few relief cuts were all it would take. She pressed the glass between her running pliers, here, there, and the edges broke away, the perfect circle left waiting for her to work her magic. She did it again to another sheet of clear glass, making a perfect match for the first one.

Cutting a half circle under her wave cut she stacked the pieces of glass matching the curved edges of the circle. She liked what she saw. In her mind, she imagined the flat pieces of glass fused together by heat, becoming a glossy painting of blues and greens then slumped into a mold forming the final bowl. She couldn't wait to see it become what it was meant to be.

Carefully she cleaned all the components, making sure no fingerprints remained.

Picking up a soft gray colored thin rod of glass, she flipped on her torch, then dipped the rod into the flame, carefully softening it so she could bend it to her will. A stylized seagull emerged from the rod. Maddy heated the edge of the wing and set it free from the remainder of the stick. She placed the soaring gull on the bowl blank, flying the bird high above the waves of blue.

Two more times, and Maddy had a trio of birds winging their way across the sky of the bowl. She stared at the flat circles, imagining the design dipped into the curves of the bowl. It was missing something. Maddy looked up at her shelf at the jars of glass crushed into fine powders and crystals like a baker's rack of decorator sugars.

Selecting a palette of reds and oranges, Maddy painted the sky of her bowl bank with the crushed glass crystals creating a sunset background for her birds.

Once she was satisfied, she donned a thin pair of cotton gloves and picked up the stacks of cut glass sheets and sprinkles. She set the stack in an empty space within the waiting kiln. Checking to make sure the birds hadn't moved she straightened, groaning as she worked out the kinks in her back. She surveyed all the other pieces waiting in the kiln for the next step. Twelve bowl blanks, all ocean scenes designed to complement each other were waiting for her to fire them into their fused state.

She consulted her notebook, checking her firing schedule for the type of glass and thickness she had loaded in the kiln. She never trusted her memory. It would be a costly mistake to enter the schedule wrong and ruin the pieces. She entered the schedule into the computer controller, the ramp up time, the top temperature, holding, and the drop in temperature, holding to anneal before the final cooling off. She wouldn't be able to see the results until the next night. Patience was a big part of being a glass artist.

The kiln started to make ticking sounds, heating up, the materials expanding. When she was certain everything was going as it should, Maddy turned and went to work cleaning up her workspace. After putting the large pieces of scrap glass away in the scrap buckets, careful to make sure they were in with the same kind of glass, she took the bench brush and carefully cleaned all the tiny shards of glass from the surface. She had learned the hard way early in her career that forgetting to sweep up the glass slivers led to a very bloody hand or two. Satisfied everything was in order, she walked toward the door, ready to leave her studio for the night. Just before she flipped off the lights, she turned her attention to the watercolor that hung next to the top of the Dutch door. It was the one Tripp had painted for her on their first anniversary of living together. The couple on the beach was obviously them, Maddy with her black hair French-braided and hanging to her waist, Tripp with his long shaggy hair lifted by the wind , his arm slung around her shoulder. The ocean was washed in the soft pastels of sunrise. Tripp had caught the moment perfectly in the transparent colors of paint.

Her heart hurt, the ache seeping into her soul.

He'd left her. He'd left Grey's Harbor. He said he needed to be in a metropolitan area. For his art. To be fair, he'd asked her to come, to follow him and their dreams, but she couldn't. She couldn't leave Grey's Harbor. She couldn't leave her cottage and her studio by the sea.

She locked the door, painted a jaunty blue, and smiled at the wren who was sitting on the sunny yellow shutters. Her studio was perfect. Had been perfect until Tripp left. Now it was empty, the studio not so sunny anymore.

"Hey, Maddy!"

She looked up to see Maeve Wynn on the dune path coming up from the beach. Maeve skirted the old ruins of a foundation and fell in step with Maddy as she left her studio and followed the path to her cottage a few steps away.

"What brings you out here this evening, Maeve? Taking a break from the diner?" Maddy smiled at her friend.

"I just needed to get away for a bit. The diner's in good hands, and I just wanted to take a walk on the beach. I lost track of time and space and never dreamed I would end up this far from town."

"Are you okay?"

"Sure, I just needed to think some things out."

"Tank driving you crazy again?" Maddy asked slyly, her hooded eyes watching her friend's expression out of the corner.

"You really are perceptive, aren't you? Must be the artist in you."

Maddy gazed out at the ocean as she stepped up to her covered back porch. She patted an old-fashioned metal scalloped-back chair painted a cheerful coral. Maeve sunk into it gratefully.

"I don't know Maeve. Tripp left, and I didn't see that coming, so I'm not as perceptive as you might think. On the other hand, my guess is you would go for a raspberry iced tea about now."

"I'll take you up on that. I could use a drink before my long hike back. Need help?" Maddy shook her head and disappeared into the tiny cottage painted to match the airy studio next to it. Maeve leaned back in the chair and sighed. Men. They certainly could complicate things.

Maddy came back out, ice tinkling in the glasses filled with the refreshing brew. The antique wooden screen door slammed behind her, a comforting sound from her childhood. She settled into a matching chair next to Maeve and they sipped their tea in comfortable silence.

"You need a dog," Maeve said suddenly.

Maddy laughed.

"What brought that on?" she asked.

"I don't know. This porch needs a pooch, and you're out here alone. Now that Tripp is gone, I don't know, I just don't like the idea of you alone."

"It's kind of peaceful," she said, sadly. "And I lived here alone before Tripp moved in, so I can do it again."

"I know, but it's quieter when someone moves out." Maeve watched the waves roll in, the tide moving the water closer while sea gulls hunted in the foam.

"You and Tank, you're okay, right?"

"I don't know. Sometimes we're so right for each other, then other times we're like oil and water. This is one of those other times."

Maeve drained her glass and stood up.

"I need to be getting back. Thanks for the tea, sweetie."

"How 'bout I drive you? I've been thinking about your lobster mac and cheese all day. I might as well get some. Nothing else will satisfy me when I have my heart set on that."

"Well, we'd better get going then, because you know I sell out of that early." Maeve grinned at her friend, happy to have the companionship and ride back to the Cathead Diner.

2

*T*ires crunched in the oyster shell drive as the headlights swept across the front of the cheerful cottage. Maddy smiled as she did every time she came home. She loved the cottage by the sea. She had summered there when she was a child when her parents unlocked the place to escape the oppressive heat of their tiny inland home. She never understood why they were able to have this special place, her family barely made ends meet, but every summer the cottage was there for them to spend endless summer nights hunting ghost crabs, flying kites, and fishing the surf. Her father and mother both set up easels on the porch of the tiny studio and painted seascapes to sell in the tourist shops up and down the coast; her mother worked in acrylics, her father watercolors. In the winter, her dad worked full time with Smith and Son's Heating and Cooling repairing errant furnaces. Her mother would clean the homes of the "haves."

Her parents still worked in the summers, but they took turns keeping an eye on her, splitting their shifts until she was old enough to fend for herself.

She stepped out of the car and picked up her box of leftovers.

Maeve had given her an extra-large helping of the decadent, creamy, cheesy pasta dish, so Maddy had plenty of food for tomorrow's lunch. She walked up the steps to the wide gracious porch and unlocked the blue door with the shiny brass handle, entering into her sanctuary of polished wooden floors and stained-glass panels hung in front of the old clear glass windows throughout the cottage. Her world was filled with sparkling, colorful light and that was just as she liked it.

She picked up the mail she had tossed carelessly on the side table earlier and sorted through it. A handful of bills, a flyer for a rummage sale at the Methodist church, and a curious thick creamy envelope of quality paper. She switched on the lamp behind the large rocking chair and settled into it to open the intriguing envelope.

Inside she found a folded card with a beautifully embossed monogram. The silvery gray ornate G filled the cover with flourishes decorated with tiny birds and intricate nests. It was a stunning work of art.

Maddy rubbed her finger over the embossing, enjoying the richness of it then opened the card and began to read the spidery handwriting. It was a request for a quote to repair several stained-glass windows which were damaged by hail from the last storm that had hit Grey's Harbor. The author understood that Maddy did exquisite work and cost was not a concern; might she stop by and provide a quote? It was signed Mirabelle Grey.

Well that explained the gray G on the front of the card and the fact that cost was not an option. One of the well-heeled Greys needed something done. Her distaste of the family was soon overshadowed by the excitement of being able to restore the windows in the beautiful old painted lady that sat on a hill overlooking the ocean just north of town. It was one of the most beautiful homes in the village. It sat up on a bluff with a view of the ocean, the property stretching to the beach. In fact, Maddy could just glimpse the tower of the house in the distance if she was at the right spot on the beach behind her cottage.

She closed her eyes trying to remember the intricate designs of the windows in that house. She had seen it a million times, admired it from afar. Pale purples and yellows came to mind, with bevels and rondelles dotting the symmetrical curvaceous design. She thought she remembered turquoise and moss green glass rectangles marching in a border around the center focal point, but she couldn't be sure. She was positive that some of the glass would be English muffle, the texture making it hard to cut, but she loved a challenge and the money would be welcome.

She leaned her head back and closed her eyes. Tripp would have been excited about this project for her. He would have grabbed her hand and pulled her to her feet, insisting that she drive him by the house so he could see these beautiful windows.

Maddy stood up and picked up her keys. Tripp would have been right. She should drive by the house and see if the windows were lit up from the inside. Stained glass was beautiful during the day, but at night, lit from behind, it was breathtaking.

Just as she had hoped, the house was ablaze with light, at least the downstairs. She drove down the quiet road slowly, wanting to be able to take in everything on one pass. The windows were more ornate than she had remembered with lots of colors and bevels. The double front doors held large panels each with a center glass piece showcasing the same intricate gray monogram that graced the card. As far as she could tell in the dark the monogramed pieces weren't damaged. She was grateful for that.

She was getting excited. This project would definitely be a challenge, and that made her smile. The curves were intricate, and the pieces were many. It was hard to tell in the dark, but it looked like several windows on the front of the house had suffered some serious damage. It made sense as the house faced west. Spring storms sweeping in from the west were common in Grey's Harbor.

It was too late to call the number listed on the card, but she would do it first thing in the morning. Her mind went to work on the drive home, thinking about how to remove the windows, transport them, and where she was going to set up a space in her tiny studio to give her enough room to work on the windows and still continue to fill the fused glass orders she had yet to create. It was a good problem to have, but it was still a problem. Tripp would have had the answers. He could have helped her handle the large windows and make space in the studio, but Tripp was gone. For good. She knew it in her heart, and there was no point wishing otherwise. She drove the last three miles home, tears running down her cheeks, her heart aching with grief.

"Call me Miss Mirabelle, dear. Everyone does. And this is Miss Maggie." The elderly woman gestured to the white standard poodle sitting calmly beside her. The poodle regarded Maddy, then blinked. "She approves of you. That's a good sign."

"Thank you?" said Maddy not sure about the exchange that was happening. She was just here to get a look at the damaged stained-glass windows to be able to prepare an estimate for the repair.

"Oh, for heaven's sake, don't look like you don't belong here. You're a Grey for God's sake!" Miss Mirabelle scolded. She turned and walked toward the sitting parlor on the left, leaving the grand hall and Maddy standing in it. "Follow me, dear, and sit."

She lowered herself, gripping the cane as she eased down onto the Victorian horsehair settee. Maddy looked around the parlor, uneasy and unaccustomed to such formalities. She spotted a wing chair next to Miss Mirabelle and lowered herself into it, uncomfortably perching on the edge, her back unaccustomedly straight.

"I'm not a Grey like you're a Grey," Maddy protested, keenly aware of the difference in their backgrounds.

Miss Mirabelle snorted. "You are most certainly a Grey like I am a Grey. Where did you get that silly notion?"

Maddy cast her eyes around the beautifully preserved Victorian home, complete with stained glass above every window and even over the entranceways to each room. The furniture looked original, *probably gracing the Grey's family's asses for generations*, she thought to herself.

"Your parents never explained your lineage, did they? Weren't you ever curious? After all, you carry the name of the town, and you know that we Grey's have populated it well. Surely you were curious about your family?"

"No, actually I wasn't. My parents told me I was an offshoot line, not one of the mighty Grey family." She caught herself and had the decency to look contrite.

"No, don't apologize. You have a point. The Grey's can be a might big for their britches. We are a proud family, but a good family. Sure, we have our assholes, oh don't look so shocked, dear. I can swear with the best of them. Yes, we have some not nice people, but what family doesn't? I'm willing to bet all of them have skeletons in the closet. Now I'm tired. I would like you to look at the damaged windows then give me a quote for the repair." She held up her hand as Maddy started to speak. "I don't expect the quote today. Shall we say the day after tomorrow? Will that give you enough time?"

Maddy thought quickly. She could probably pull that together as long as her suppliers would be able to give her a glass match for each sample and a solid quote per sheet. She nodded at the elderly woman who was peering at her keenly over her glasses.

"Then, when you come back, we will have a spot of tea. I suspect by that time your curiosity will have gotten the best of you, and you will be ready to ask why you get to live in that cottage by the ruined foundation of Grey's Landing. Come on, Miss Maggie. It's time to retire for our nap."

With that the old woman rose on her creaky knees leaving Maddy standing in the parlor, her mouth hanging slightly open.

Weird, she thought as she pulled out her tape measure and note pad and began assessing the hail damage to the beautiful stained-glass windows.

*B*ack at her studio, she studied the pictures she took of the damaged windows. The color match was going to be tricky. Her glass supplier specialized in restoration glass, but that was never a sure thing. The colors in these windows were especially rich.

She crossed to the little desk in the corner and turned on the computer. She needed to work quickly in order to provide a reasonable quote the day after tomorrow. If she wasn't careful, she could end up losing her shirt on this deal.

Maddy settled into the desk chair and stared out the window as she waited for the computer to boot up. It was a gray day and the ocean was angry. She loved the sound of the pounding surf but didn't like the dull color of the ocean today. It seemed like ever since Tripp left, the world was lifeless and gray. She needed some sunshine to light up her stained glass and bring joy to her world.

Her computer beeped announcing an email. It was up and running. Ignoring her inbox, she began to peruse her glass supplier's website, looking for the right colors and textures to use for the repairs to Miss Mirabelle's windows. She took notes and wrote down stock numbers, making the list, more and more encouraged as she worked.

A sharp knock startled Maddy. Looking up, she saw Ryker Wynn poking his head through the top open half of her Dutch door. His incredible green eyes crinkled at the corners as he peered in the studio looking for her.

"Come on in, Ryker," she invited as she stood, stretching her back.

"Working hard?" he asked glancing at her computer. "The kiln seems cold."

"Putting together a quote," she said, "and yeah, it's time to open up that kiln and see if the magic happened or a disaster."

"How often does disaster happen?" Ryker teased. "I'm guessing not often, or you wouldn't be such a successful glass artist." He crossed the studio and gave her a quick hug.

Maddy smiled at him and moved toward the kiln. She wrapped her hands around the lid handle and tilted it up exposing bowl blanks, each one no longer stacks but fused into colorful discs. Her practiced eye scanned the contents looking for problems while she questioned Ryker.

"So, what brings you out to my little slice of beach?" She poked a finger into the kiln and ran it over the three seagulls she had set in the sky. Everything was smooth, no bubbles, no cracks. Life was good.

"Those are gorgeous, Maddy. They're going to be bowls, right?" Ryker asked as he imagined what they would look like on a table or shelf, the light filtering through and lighting up the colors.

"Yeah. They're for an order from an upscale restaurant in Nag's Head. Only have twenty-four more to go."

She grimaced at the thought and then smiled as she remembered the amount she was invoicing that restaurant owner.

"I'm guessing it's a good problem to have."

"It is, but I'm anxious to get started on my new project." She looked at him expectantly knowing he would ask what it was.

"Actually, to answer your question of what brings me here, it's your new little project."

She looked at him confused.

He laughed.

"You don't think you were going to remove those windows from Mirabelle Grey's house and haul them here by yourself, did you?"

Maddy's cheeks colored.

"Yeah, I was trying to work through that in my head but figured I would deal with it later."

"You don't have to deal with it. I have been doing some repair work out there on the house and Miss Mirabelle asked if I would be willing to do the removal and install under your direction. So, I'm at your disposal."

Ryker ran a very successful contracting business. He was Maeve Wynn's brother and Tank Harmon's best friend. Tank worked for Ryker and dated his sister in an on again off again fashion. Maddy had grown up with all of them.

"Okay, but the thought of Tank handling those delicate panes of glass makes my palms sweat."

"Aw, Maddy, Tank may look all big and rough, but he's as gentle as a kitten," Ryker assured her.

Maddy's brain conjured up an image of the good looking muscle bound guy and gentle isn't what came to mind. Dangerous, yes. Hot, absolutely. Gentle, not a chance.

"Have I ever let you down? Or has Tank for that matter?" he asked, his right eyebrow raised.

"No, Ryker, you never have. I haven't been impressed with some of your life decisions, but I'll let that go," she teased him, thinking about his choices in women. Ryker was like a brother to her, and she was very protective of him. She also had no trouble calling him on his mistakes and stupid choices.

"Leave my love life out of this," he warned. "So, just let me know when you're ready to remove and transport, and we'll be at your service. Oh, and let me know if you have suggestions as to how to pack them for the move. I'll do whatever you tell me. Besides, I don't want to get on Mirabelle Grey's bad side. Not good juju."

"No kidding," she agreed. She had the feeling that Mirabelle Grey was still powerful despite her feeble appearance. Maddy didn't trust the old women's attempt at familiarity the other day. Just because Maddy's last name was Grey didn't mean she had anything to do with the Grey family or the Grey legacy. She was just Maddy, and that's the way she liked it and wanted to keep it.

4

"*I* think you'll find everything you need in the quote. Once you go over it, I'll be happy to answer any questions you might have."

Miss Mirabelle waved her glittering hand, dismissing Maddy's practiced speech with her ring encrusted fingers.

"I'm sure it's fine, dear. I'll forward it to my accountant so he'll know what to expect and when to issue you drafts. I assume you will need a down payment in order to secure supplies. He will be contacting you tomorrow to make the necessary arrangements. Now follow me please, we have things to discuss."

Miss Mirabelle turned abruptly and made her way deeper into the great hall, once again leaving Maddy standing with her mouth open.

That didn't go the way it was supposed to, Maddy thought. *I lost control of the conversation. Damn it.* She had been determined not to let Mirabelle take over, but of course, she did.

"This way dear." Mirabelle stomped her cane impatiently demanding Maddy follow.

Maddy sighed and made her way down the great hall, past the grand staircase and into the large, ornate dining room. She hesitated for a minute, looking around to see where Miss Mirabelle had disappeared to.

"In here," Mirabelle called. Maddy followed her voice to a small room off the dining room. It was a beautifully appointed ladies' sitting room. A silver tea service graced a low table, and Miss Mirabelle was already seated waiting to pour. A tray of tiny sandwiches with their crusts removed were waiting for them as well. *I'd prefer a burger,* Maddy thought, until she spied the scones. *Damn,* she was won over.

"I assume your family raised you properly," said Miss Mirabelle as she splashed some milk into a teacup, then poured steaming tea on top of it. "This is the finest Welsh brew. Sugar?" she asked as she handed the cup over.

Maddy looked at the creamy cup of tea, memories of her childhood flooding back. Vague wisps of memories of a tiny white table splashed with color. More vivid ones with her mother and father playing tea party with a delicate china child-sized tea set as they sat on the back porch, the sea lapping at the beach. She smiled and accepted the cup. She hadn't had Welsh tea in years.

"Thank you. It's been a long time, and it smells delicious." Maddy waited until her hostess had her cup prepared, then Maddy took a sip. The tea was simply exquisite. It was definitely a finer brew of tea than her family had ever had the privilege of sipping.

Miss Mirabelle offered Maddy the sandwiches and scones, looking pleased with herself.

"So, you do embrace your Welsh heritage and your Grey lineage," she stated, her dark eyes boring into her soul. "You certainly have the look."

Maddy suddenly became conscious of her long curly black hair and smoky black-brown eyes. The contrast of her pale skin against her dark features was striking. Combine that with her full lips and delicate facial structure and she was an absolute beauty. Maddy never recognized that side of herself, usually tossing her hair in a ponytail or tucking it under a hat and shrugging off the makeup that could accentuate her features. Maddy just wanted to be Maddy, so she always played down her looks. She wanted to be recognized for her brains, her artistic ability, and her work ethic, not some arrangement of DNA.

Mirabelle gestured to a portrait that hung above an ornate ceramic fireplace. Maddy followed her gaze. She was looking at a painting that had an uncanny resemblance to herself had she ever dressed in a green lace formal that dipped down her forearms showcasing her creamy shoulders. Maddy glanced back at Mirabelle.

"You?" she asked.

Mirabelle nodded.

"You were beautiful." *Oh damn, I just stuck my foot in my mouth again.* "I mean, you are beautiful," she stammered.

"Rubbish," Mirabelle snorted. "I'm an old woman with an old woman's looks, but yes, in my day, I could hold my own." She smiled remembering the glittering parties and the suitors, all long gone in a cobweb of memories.

"You carry the Grey genes my dear, even if you don't want to admit it."

"I'm the poor relation, Miss Mirabelle. My family has had nothing to do with your family or your relatives. We have never been part of your family." She was getting hot, her temper flaring.

"And you have the Grey temper, too, I see." Miss Mirabelle just smiled and sipped her tea.

Maddy picked up a scone and nibbled it, thinking. *What was Miss Mirabelle's point? What was she trying to prove?*

"Madeline, surely you're a bit curious. After all, you're creative, an artist. Inquisitiveness comes with that package."

Maddy's good sense began to take over. This woman was going to pay her to repair the hail damaged stained glass. Her practiced eye had noticed some other work that needed to be done to some of the glass on the inside of the house. She could parlay this into a very profitable venture. Perhaps she should amuse this wealthy old woman and pretend to actually care. She didn't, she reminded herself. She wasn't interested in being associated with the "haves" that her mother had cleaned for, but she wasn't opposed to taking their money.

"I suppose I wouldn't mind being entertained with a good story. That is if there is a story to be told."

"Oh Madeline, my dear, there most certainly is a marvelous story to be told." Her eyes glittered in anticipation.

"And my name is Maddy, not Madeline."

"Your birth certificate says Madeline, whether you like it or not, but I will respect you and call you by your nickname, common as it is." Miss Mirabelle snorted with laughter knowing that she had gotten to Maddy with the dig.

Maddy just smiled and sipped her tea. There was a lot of money at stake, so she prepared herself to just sit back and be bored by an old lady's gossip.

Miss Mirabelle studied the girl with practiced eyes. She recognized the self-sufficient nature, the proud demeanor of a girl who grew up pinching pennies, and the distain for the people who had and who looked down on those who didn't. Mirabelle sighed. Her family had done so much good for this village, founded it, grew it, supported it, even bailed out the inhabitants with charity when they needed it, but they were a proud family, proud of their line, and paternity was important.

"I'm certain you know the story of Madeline Aubuchon,"

"Of course, everyone knows that she was pregnant, and she threw herself off the lighthouse into the sea killing herself. She haunts the lighthouse to this day searching for her baby."

"Yes, that is true, except for the haunting part. That remains to be seen. What most people, at least people today don't know is that the baby was cut from her womb and given to another to raise."

"Wait, cut from her womb? Like someone performed a C-section on her? She didn't die in the ocean?"

"Oh no, she most certainly died. She drowned, but Zachariah Grey ordered the baby to be cut from her to save it. You see the baby was a bastard Grey."

Maddy winced at the word and the way Mirabelle said it, so matter of fact.

"Oh, don't look so offended. It's a fact. Madeline Aubuchon was not married to Cooper Grey, but he fathered her child. Zachariah Grey would not permit that child to be part of the inheritance line, but the old goat had a heart, so he placed the child with a woman in the village who had lost a child, to be raised by her, but he allowed the child to carry the Grey surname. He also made certain that the woman and the child led a decent life."

"The life of a poor relation," Maddy snorted with disdain.

"Cooper Grey made some poor choices. Ones he knew would have ramifications."

"He could have done the right thing and married her," Maddy said, the scone she had just bitten turning dry in her mouth.

"Yes, he could have and should have, I suppose, but we can't change the past." Mirabelle tsked.

"No, not good enough. Why didn't he marry her? Why wasn't she good enough for him?"

"Well, the truth is ugly," Mirabelle sighed. "She wasn't of the quality Cooper was seeking. She was a distracting beauty, but she didn't come from money. She gave of herself hoping to elevate herself, but he was not interested in making her his wife."

"So, she fell in love with a rich boy, but was from the wrong side of the tracks, so his parents put an end to it, and he was spineless and didn't do what was right," Maddy filled in.

"Actually, no. You have the spineless part right, but Zachariah had urged Cooper to do the right thing. He had suspected that the Aubuchon girl was pregnant with his son's child, but his son denied it. She had a reputation, so the question was reasonable, I suppose. When she named his son as the father with her dying breath, Zachariah did what he thought was best. The rest is history."

"Okay, so that's a sad story, and I feel horrible for her, but why tell me this story on this day?"

"Because, my dear, you are a descendent of Cooper Grey. These windows you are going to be working on should be yours."

5

*M*iss Mirabelle sipped her tea, clearly enjoying the look of shock on the young woman's face. She waited for the shock to turn to anger, but it didn't happen. She almost wished it would. She didn't delight in the look of bewilderment that had settled over the pretty girl.

"Miss Mirabelle, there are a lot of Greys. These windows, this house wouldn't have been mine."

"But they would have." Mirabelle paused, waiting to deliver the final knife stabbing revelation. "Maddy, dear. I am a descendent of Cooper's second son, Bevyn. So, you see, you're the one entitled to this wealth." She waited for that to sink in.

Maddy calmly drained her tea and patted her mouth. Her mind was racing. *How exactly should she handle this information. Just what was Mirabelle expecting of her, wanting her to do?* She carefully settled her face, keeping it devoid of emotion. After all, what was done was done and really meant nothing to her.

"Well, thank you for the story. It was definitely entertaining, and thank you for the tea and snacks." Her lips turned up at the word, knowing it was a crass word for such a lovely spread. "But I have a lot of work to do, so if the contract is to your liking, you can sign it and I can get to work, or you can look it over and get it to me at your leisure. I have some glass in the kiln and I'd like to get back to my studio.

Miss Mirabelle smiled, recognizing the proud girl's attempt at control and normalcy.

"I'm certain that the contract is acceptable, but I will look it over and have it sent to your studio by tomorrow with the down payment draft. And Maddy, thank you for kindly joining me at tea and listening to me unburden my soul." She sought the girl's eyes hoping that Maddy would see the sincerity in her.

Maddy's heart did not thaw. She was not absolving this woman of any guilt. Maddy had nothing to do with this and she just wanted to leave.

She crossed the room and turned at the doorway.

"I'll let myself out. Thank you again." She tried not to look at the proud woman who was still sitting there. She tried not to notice that those ancient eyes were misted and touched with sadness.

As she walked through the huge dining hall Miss Maggie approached her, regarding her with liquid brown eyes, wagging her tail slightly.

"Hi girl," Maddy said, lifting her hand to the dog's nose. Maggie sniffed her fingers then allowed Maddy to scratch behind her ears. Her tail wagged then stilled. Maggie perked her ears and moved away, trotting to the little sitting room where Maddy had left her mistress.

On the way out Maddy stopped to look at the windows again. She was glad Ryker was going to help remove and transport them. This was going to be one hell of a job.

*

*M*addy drove past the road that led to her cottage and she headed into town. She was trying to process everything that was in her head and she didn't want to be alone. Thoughts of Tripp played in her mind. How she wished she could tell him about the story Mirabelle told. Sighing, she glanced to her left, taking in the ocean and the beach as she drove the coast road. The lighthouse rose from the dunes in the distance, the legacy of Grey's Harbor, the marker of Madeline's death. Crazy, she thought. As kids they would build fires on the beach then sneak to the lighthouse, keeping hidden from view so the keeper wouldn't see. They would scare each other with stories of the ghost of the woman who had died there, who haunted the place. Some nights, when the winds were high and the seas rough, they would swear they could hear her crying for her child. It was always good for a healthy scare and a teenage snuggle after.

Now all she felt was sadness as she drove, the lighthouse receding in her side mirror. She couldn't imagine the pain that woman must have felt to have taken her own life and the life of her child, the child she didn't know had lived, had grown, had fathered sons, one of those descendants fathering her.

Parking in front of Anna's Bakery, Maddy slipped out of her car. She was craving sweets and on the prowl. What she really wanted was some chocolate butter pecan ice cream from Daisy's Ice Cream Shop, but Daisy's was no longer. A crime in Maddy's book. It couldn't be helped. Some people just didn't feel the need to stay in Grey's Harbor. Her heart hitched as she thought of Tripp. Well, if she couldn't drown her thoughts in a decadent, creamy ice cream wonder from Daisy's, she could at least get some Cinnamon Crunch muffins from Anna's and then head across the street for one of Maeve's malts.

The shop bell tinkled merrily as Maddy pushed the door to the bakery open. She was greeted with the heady smells of yeast and sugar. That smell always took her back to the days when her daddy drove into town to pick up kerosene or seed packets from the hardware store. He would take her hand when they left and look down at her seriously.

"All that work deserves a donut, don't you think?"

"And one for Mommy, too?" Maddy would ask, her eyes sparkling with joy.

"Of course, but maybe a cinnamon muffin for her."

Anna was younger then but still white-haired and plump. Her soft blue eyes would crinkle at the corners as she would watch the young girl seriously consider the different donuts. After all the thought, she usually ended up with a raised donut covered in a thick layer of chocolate frosting. Anna usually slipped two in for the price of one.

"Hello, Maddy," Anna said, glancing up at the clock. "What brings you in at closing time? That's not your normal routine?" she said, not unkindly.

"I know, but I just needed a sweet. I'm sure you're out of chocolate frosted donuts and cinnamon crunch muffins," Maddy said sadly, glancing into the depleted case.

"Now you know those go early. I have a bran muffin, but I don't think that's what you have in mind." Anna laughed softly, then sobered as she saw the look in Maddy's eyes.

"Maddy, honey, what ails you today? You look all out of sorts."

"Did you know that I was related to Miss Mirabelle Grey?" she blurted. She snapped her mouth closed, shocked that is what came from her.

Anna tsked and crossed through the swinging gate, coming around to the front of the counter. She took one look at Maddy and wrapped her in generous arms, pulling the girl close to her ample body.

Maddy, unable to contain her sadness, let the dam go, tears flooding her eyes.

"Finding this out isn't the only thing that's making you sad, is it girl? Tripp is still hurting your heart, isn't he?"

Maddy gulped and nodded, feeling helpless as a child.

"Well look at the time," said Anna and she moved Maddy over to one of the tiny tables that graced the corner of the little bakery. She crossed to the door and flipped the sign to closed, locking them into the sweet sanctuary.

"You sit right there, dear, and compose your thoughts. I'll be right back."

Anna ambled to the back room while Maddy dug in her purse to find a tissue to wipe her tears and dab her nose.

Within minutes, Anna came back carrying two steaming mugs of cocoa dressed with mounds of whipped cream and garnished with shaved dark chocolate. She disappeared again and came back with two plates each with a generous slice of warm cinnamon coffee cake.

"Oh Anna, you didn't have to do this. Please, let me pay…"

"You hush, child. You're not a customer right now. You're a friend. Now have a sip of that cocoa. It'll heal what ails you."

Maddy picked up the warm mug, the heat melting into her hands like a warm hug. She brought the mug to her lips, blew and then sipped. Her eyes opened with surprise.

"Oh my, Anna. This is delicious. Hazelnut…" She said savoring the flavor with her second sip.

"Yes, the flavor is hazelnut. That cocoa has a healthy shot of Frangelico, just to be social." Anna smiled and tipped her mug to her mouth, enjoying the delicious drink. Then she nodded to the coffee cake. "Eat it while it's warm. I suspect you haven't had dinner, but dessert is always better first."

Maddy nodded, her eyes lighting up with merriment.

"True confessions. I had scones at Mirabelle's this afternoon, too. I've really eaten nothing but sweets, and Frangelico laced cocoa is a sin of my youth."

"Ah, so that's why Mirabelle needed those scones today. Was quite insistent that I make them and have them delivered this morning. Now I know what the special occasion was. She decided to unburden her soul I take it. But why are you involved with Mirabelle in the first place?"

"Some of the stained-glass windows were damaged in the last hail-storm. She hired me to do the repairs. I'm excited to do it. I love restoring old stained-glass. I just didn't know this job would come with baggage."

"And you have enough to deal with healing your broken heart," Anna said wisely.

"Yeah, I guess," Maddy whispered. "Why did she decide now was the time to tell me that I am the descendent of an illegitimate Grey? Why does any of that matter?"

"Honey, she's old. She's alone. Do you know she was unable to have children, and she is the last of her line of Greys, of the Cooper Greys?"

"So, all of the sudden she wants a granddaughter? Not gonna happen," Maddy said, her voice sounding angrier than she intended.

Anna smiled and nodded to the cocoa.

"Have some more of that. It's calming to the soul."

Maddy had the decency to look sheepish.

"I'm sorry, Anna. I've just got a lot swirling around in my mind. There are so many questions..." Her voice trailed off.

"My guess is some of those questions you don't really want to ask because you might not like the answer."

Maddy considered what Anna said.

"I think you might be right," she whispered.

"Maddy, you're a grown woman. You have a right to ask questions of anything you want, and you also have the right not to. Sometimes it's better to let sleeping dogs lie. Then you don't have to deal with what happens when they wake up. On the other hand, if you miss an opportunity, you may never get it back. Only you can make that decision."

Maddy stared at the last bite of coffee cake. Did she want to know any more than what Mirabelle had told her? Did she really want to know what her parents had not told her? Had they willingly withheld the truth from her and for what reason? Just thinking about it made her head hurt. Or maybe it was all the sweets.

"I don't know Anna. I guess I'm going to have to let this stew for a little bit. I do know that if I don't eat some real food instead of all these sweets, I might be ill. Do you want to go to the Cathead with me?" Maddy asked.

"No, thank you for asking, but I have plans for tonight," Anna said, blushing a little.

"Going to sit with Clarence for a bit on his boat?" Maddy teased, referring to the village Casanova who lived on a houseboat at Cadigan's Marina.

Anna began to blush furiously.

"Oh my gosh, Anna. I was only joking," Maddy said, apologizing, but then realized that she hit on something. "Wait, you're seeing Clarence? Good for you, Anna. That's great," she said sincerely. "Hell, maybe I should go see him, too."

Anna rose to clear to dishes and gave Maddy a swat on the arm.

"Go on, get outta here before I spank you for impudence." Then she smiled and shook her head as Maddy started to help. "No, go on. Think about what we talked about, but don't take too long. Sometimes opportunities are missed with indecision." She kissed Maddy on the cheek and nodded toward the door. "Just turn the key to unlock it and let yourself out. Have a good evening, my dear."

6

*M*addy changed her mind. She could see that there was a lull in the dinner crowd at the Cathead, and she suddenly felt the rare need to be surrounded by people, so she got in her car, deciding to drive to the Mizzen Mast instead. If she was lucky, a local musician might be playing there. A little music and some of Izzy's bar food just might be the ticket.

When she pulled into the gravel parking lot, she caught site of Ryker and Tank sitting on the back deck drinking beer and contemplating the river.

"Hey guys," she called as she stepped up to the large, festive wooden deck flanking the river that flowed lazily past on its way to the ocean.

"Hey, Mad." Tank rose and crushed her in his bicep bound arms.

"Easy, Tank," she squealed, feeling squeezed to death, but protected at the same time.

He looked down at her, studying her. Despite his he-man outward appearance, Tank was perceptive. He always knew what was going on, but sometimes he just didn't act on it the way others would expect. Hence the on again off again with Maeve.

"You're not looking so good, darlin'," he drawled. "Beer or something harder?" He rose to get her something at the bar.

"Actually, I don't know what I want. I need some food, that's for sure. Are you guys eating and can a girl join you, or is this boy's night?"

"Maddy, even if it were boy's night, you've always been one of us. We haven't ordered dinner yet, so sit down and join us."

"Thanks," she said gratefully. "I really didn't want to be alone right now. I'm going to run to the ladies' room." She kissed Tank's cheek, inviting him to sit back down, and gave Ryker a half hug on the way into the Mizzen Mast proper.

Ryker watched as she walked away from them.

"That girl is hurting," he said, anger touching his voice.

"Tripp didn't do her any favors, that's for sure," Tank agreed. "You know, I never really liked that guy. He seemed like he was always out for himself. He never put Maddy first, so I wasn't surprised when he left."

"He did ask her to come with him," Ryker reminded Tank.

"He did, but you notice that invitation didn't come with a ring." Tank grumbled.

"Like the ring you haven't put on my sister's finger, yet?" Ryker teased his friend. They had played this conversation before, many times.

"Exactly, just like that," agreed Tank, "but I haven't asked her to give up her life and her business either without that kind of commitment. I wouldn't do that to her. I care about her too much."

"I know. I also know you two are like oil and water. Sometimes you are great together and other times you separate. I just wish you'd figure it all out."

"Tell that to that sister of yours. She can be a hot head.'

"No shit," said Ryker as he raised his beer to his best friend. "Just don't hurt her or I'll have to beat the shit out of you."

Tank flexed his muscles and Ryker smirked.

"Are you two fixin' to mess my place up?"

"Nope, Izzy. We'll be well-behaved gentlemen," Tank promised solemnly.

"Well, don't hurt yourself being something you're not. I just don't want you busting up my chairs." She grinned down at them. "I saw Maddy going into the ladies' room. She joining you?"

"It looks like it. Put whatever she's drinking on my bill," Ryker said, draining his beer and looking at Izzy expectantly.

"No problem. Are you boys expecting someone else to join you, cause there's some guy in the bar asking for you, Ryker."

Ryker glanced toward the door just in time to see Brett Mason pointing him out to a tall bearded man clad in jeans and a rolled-sleeve flannel. The man shook Brett's hand then walked confidently over to Ryker's table.

Izzy walked away to attend other customers.

Ryker stayed seated, not sure who this guy was. Tank was wary. The man extended his hand to Ryker and settled a smile on his face.

"Ryker Wynn?" the man asked. "Jaxx Stockman" he said, not waiting for Ryker's answer.

Ryker shook his hand and indicated Jaxx could sit.

"What can I do for you, Mr. Stockman?"

"You can hire me," he said confidently.

Tank snorted. This was gonna be good.

"And why would I do that?" Ryker asked in good humor. No sense being rude to the guy.

"Because I'm a good carpenter, a hard worker, loyal, trustworthy, and my dog, Betty likes to eat."

Ryker couldn't help but smile with that. Even Tank had to grin.

"How big is this dog, Betty?" Ryker asked, curious.

"Well, sir, she's a bull mastiff, weighing in at one hundred and fifty pounds, so feeding her is kinda like feeding a family of four."

"You named a bull mastiff, Betty?" Tank asked, finally breaking his silence. "And she hasn't eaten your face off?"

"Nah, I'm a charmer, and she's good-natured." He answered with an easy smile.

Maddy walked up carrying an innocent looking iced tea.

Jaxx immediately stood.

Maddy looked shocked at the gesture. Flustered she waved him into a chair, then stood awkwardly, feeling like she may have disrupted something.

Tank pulled out the chair next to him and pulled her into it. He watched the way Jaxx was looking at Maddy with interest, the man's brown eyes darkening. It was at that minute that Tank recognized just how good looking this guy was.

"Hello, ma'am," Jaxx said, all Southern charm and good manners. "I'm Jaxx Stockman."

"Maddy Grey."

"Town namesake?" he asked, realizing his error too late as her face darkened with thunderclouds.

"No, not at all. Not really related," she said hotly, surprising Ryker and Tank. They exchanged a glance. There was more to Maddy's mood than missing her ex-boyfriend. Someone had pissed her off good.

"Well it's nice to meet you, not-really-related Maddy."

Chastened, Maddy reached her hand out to Jaxx.

"Let's start again," she said. "I'm sorry for biting your head off. I'm Maddy and a friend of Ryker and Tank."

"I'm Jaxx, and I'm new in town. I hope I'm the new employee of Mr. Wynn here, but that remains to be seen." He smiled sweetly.

Ryker admired the man's moxie, but Ryker wasn't stupid. He vetted all his employees carefully. Ryker was trusted in the homes of the wealthy inhabitants of this town. He wouldn't risk that no matter how confidently someone presented themselves.

"Stop by my office tomorrow and fill out an application. Once I look over that, and if I'm interested in hiring you, I'll have to run a background check on you, and you'll have to take a drug test. If any of that will be a problem, don't waste your time or mine filling out the paperwork." Ryker looked at the man steadily.

Jaxx met his eyes calmly, not breaking

"I'll be there first thing in the morning, sir. Now I'll leave you to enjoy your evening with this lovely lady. It was a pleasure to meet you,

Maddy." He shook both men's hands and made his way out of the bar, nodding to Izzy on the way out.

"Okay, who was that long tall drink of water," Izzy asked when she came back to take their dinner order.

"Why Izzy, this might be the first time I get to tell you about someone in this town," Ryker said with satisfaction.

Izzy, the owner of the Mizzen Mast had the ear of everyone in the village, so she was a wealth of knowledge and gossip. Despite the fact that everyone told her everything, she did not repeat it.

Izzy was trusted.

"Spill it," she said as she sat down, taking a load off.

Ryker quickly brought her up to date, Maddy quietly listening to the story, sipping her tea.

Once Izzy was satisfied, she took everyone's order, Maddy settling on a chicken quesadilla. As Izzy got up to leave Maddy stopped her.

"Iz, can you make that with extra cheese?"

"Sure honey, and I'll bring you another drink, too. You want that with extra, too?" She looked at Maddy, compassion filling her face. Damn that girl was hurting. One more drink, a double, but that was it, and Ryker or Tank was going to drive her home.

"Yeah, a double."

As Izzy left, Tank looked confused at Maddy's iced tea.

"Whatcha got in there?" he asked, picking up the drink and sniffing it.

"Iced tea with iced tea flavored vodka."

"Stealth drinking, huh?" asked Ryker as he took the new beer from the passing waitress.

"Yeah, I guess." She looked into her drink and swirled the ice cubes.

Ryker and Tank exchanged glances.

"Maddy, do you want to talk?"

"Thanks, but no. I just want to be around friends and listen to music and just forget about stuff. Is that okay? If I'm bringing you guys down, I'm sorry. I can go sit in the bar and hang with Iz."

"No, Maddy. Hang with us. It's all good. By the way, did you hear that Wayne Richards cut off Rodney Kern's big toe?"

"Wait, what?"

"Yep. Screwing around while cutting wood. Why the hell Rodney didn't have shoes on is a mystery."

7

*M*addy woke to the sun streaming in her windows, colored light from the stained-glass panels dancing across her bed.

She groaned.

True to her word, Izzy cut her off after the double, and Tank and Ryker drove her home. And she invited them in because her mother raised her right.

Tank raided her cabinet and found a bottle of rum and Maddy brewed more tea. Together, the three of them sat on the back porch and watched the moon over the ocean while they drank rum laced iced tea into the wee hours of the morning.

She rolled over. *Damn her head hurt. Why did she smell coffee?*

She sat up. *Oops. Not a good plan.*

She lay back down.

"Good morning, sunshine." Tank came into her bedroom carrying a mug of steaming coffee.

"What are you still doing here?" she asked, her throat gravely, her breath atrocious.

"Ryker and I spent the night on the deck. It was a beautiful night."

"Spent the night or passed out?" she asked.

"Honey, you're a light-weight. We're not. Your car is in the driveway safe and sound. Once I make sure you're up and okay, I'm going to work. Ryker is already setting up the crew. We're pouring the basement for a new house up in the Shore Haven subdivision. The damn owner wants to watch. Lord woman, go brush your teeth." He goaded her into standing.

He watched her critically as she made her way to the bathroom. She was motoring her way in a relatively straight line. He heard the water turn on and the sound of teeth being scrubbed. He waited, still holding the mug of coffee. Nope, the toothpaste didn't make her sick. She'd be okay. The toilet flushed and he heard her washing her hands. She came back and smiled sweetly.

"My breath will no longer slay a dragon, and I will happily take that cup of coffee, please. You're a superhero, Tank. Thanks."

"No worries, kid. Ryker and I will always take care of you. You're like a sister to us, and we'll protect you until the day we die."

She took the mug from him and leaned her head into his shoulder. His outward appearance was so tough, so impenetrable, but his heart was so kind. Maeve was a lucky girl if they could just figure out how not to push each other's buttons.

"Thanks. Now get going. Ryker is going to need you to intimidate the homeowner. I owe you guys."

She took a sip of the coffee. It was strong, just like she liked it. Then she pushed Tank out of her bedroom.

"You don't owe us anything, but lunch would be nice." He grinned as he turned to leave, shutting the front door to the cottage behind him.

Maddy padded out to the back porch and settled into one of the metal chairs. The morning chill made the chair cold on her butt. *How the hell had Ryker and Tank spent the night out here?* Tank had to have been pulling her leg.

She finished her coffee while watching the horizon and thinking about her current situation. She missed Tripp terribly. She didn't like being totally alone. In high school, her small gang of close friends was always around her. As an adult, she always had her friends. She didn't like crowds or casual acquaintances, but her tribe was always there. Then Tripp. When he came, she became exclusively his. In fact, he encouraged her to only spend time with him. He called it immersing themselves in each other. At first her friends continued to invite her to go out, to beg her and Tripp to join them, but the more she turned them down, the more isolated she had become. She didn't particularly like what she had done without even realizing it, but now it was abundantly clear. She was alone. Yet, her friends last night came through. They were there for her, like they had always been.

Yep, she would bring Ryker and Tank lunch, and she would mend some fences, but first she needed a shower, and she needed to spend an hour or so in the studio preparing some more bowl blanks.

Shaking off the slight headache, she went into the house to set the empty mug on the counter and went to get ready to face the day.

*A*s Maddy walked the short distance to her studio, she smiled and tilted her head to the sun. Just yesterday she had been lamenting that the days had been gray, but today the sun decided to shine, and it was glorious. As she unlocked the little building and stepped inside, she marveled at the riotous colors of the stained glass. All through the studio, dozens of panels of stained glass that she had designed hung from the exposed beams. The current angle of the sun was causing explosions of color on two of the walls. It was dazzling. It made her heart soar. Maddy pulled her cell phone out of her back pocket and took a couple of quick pictures, hoping it would do the scene justice. Sometimes you just couldn't catch the light.

She powered up her computer and checked the kiln while she waited for the old laptop to boot up.

The blanks she had set into the molds had slumped beautifully during the last firing. She always marveled when a firing was a success. So many things could go wrong. She removed each bowl, inspecting it for flaws. They were perfect. They would need to be photographed then carefully packed away to wait to be delivered.

She turned back to her computer and quickly checked her emails. Then she uploaded the pictures of the morning light in her studio from her phone to her social media, connecting with her clients, bringing them into her world. Immediately, the ooh ahh responses started flowing. She responded to a few then signed off. She had glass to cut.

An hour and a half later, and three bowl blanks completed, she stepped out of her studio, ready to get lunch together for the guys. As she crossed to her cottage, a large black sedan pulled in her driveway.

A man unfolded himself from the driver's seat and approached her with a tight smile on his face.

"Can I help you?" Maddy asked, suddenly feeling vulnerable. She didn't like the demeanor of this guy.

"I have a delivery for you," the man said, almost distastefully. "I am John Lavish, Miss Mirabelle Grey's attorney. Here is your signed copy of your contract to complete the repair to the damaged windows. Miss Grey also required me to provide you with funds so that you can start work immediately. I think you will find it all in order." He stared at her for a minute before handing over the envelope.

"Thank you," she said politely, but not warmly. *What was the deal with guy?*

"I'm going to speak freely. I know that Miss Grey discussed with you your lineage. She imagines that you are connected to her in some remote way. If you have found this connection intriguing and wish to pursue it for monetary gain, I must warn you that Miss Grey's considerable wealth is not designed to transfer to you upon her death."

Maddy drew a sharp breath and pulled her tiny frame up as tall as she was able.

"You can kindly leave my property, Mr. Lavish. You're insulting and out of line. I'm not interested in anything Mirabelle Grey has. I'm only interested in restoring some historic, lovely windows to their former beauty. You'll find me professional and really quite good at what I do but let me make myself clear. I do not work for you. I do not know you. I do not care for you, and I have nothing to say to you.

Now please excuse yourself, I have things to attend to that are far more important than wasting my time with someone the likes of you."

She turned and walked away careful to not appear upset. She left him standing in the driveway with his mouth set in a grim line. He was not accustomed to being spoken to in that manner. He was a powerful attorney and had connections to everyone who mattered in Grey's Harbor. No one, especially a maid's daughter had ever spoken to him like that. He would protect Mirabelle Grey's assets from that gold digger, that was for sure.

He got in his car and drove away, a little too fast for a man who was always in control. Maddy smiled as she watched from behind the stained-glass panel that hung in the window beside the front door. Despite his power suit, he had lost the upper hand a little. *From little ol' me*, she thought, satisfied.

Earlier in the day, while working on her glass, she had felt sorry for Mirabelle. The woman was alone, except for her dog. That had to be hard. Maddy herself was feeling the effects of loneliness. She had planned on making a concerted effort to be nice to the old bat when she came in contact with her at the house, but if this was any indication of the kind of treatment she was going to receive from now on, she was going to rethink her attitude toward one of the Grande Dames of the Grey clan.

Determined not to let Lavish ruin her day, she retrieved her keys, set a smile on her face, and drove into Grey's Harbor proper. The first stop was Anna's Bakery. She was hoping to see Anna there. She wanted to ask her how her evening was and to thank her for being a good friend, but she was nowhere to be seen. The lady at the counter selected six large submarine buns that had been baked that morning and put them in a white bakery bag for Maddy. At the last minute, Maddy included a dozen chocolate chip cookies. She smiled as she made her way out of the bakery and walked to the small grocery store next to the barber shop. She bought freshly sliced salami, some capicola ham, sandwich pepperoni and some sliced provolone. Everything else she would need she had at home.

She glanced at her watch. She was going to have to get a move on if she wanted to deliver the subs in time for the guys' lunch break.

She stopped back at home and quickly assembled the sandwiches, adding some sliced red onion and lettuce. She remembered at the last minute that neither Ryker nor Tank liked tomatoes. She loaded a shopping bag with the sandwiches, cookies, a bag of crab seasoned potato chips, and a bottle of sub dressing. Snagging a small cooler from a cabinet, she added some icepacks and a selection of sodas. She left the house whistling a tune. *Maybe,* she thought, *I'm beginning to heal.*

8

*M*addy pulled into the posh subdivision and wound her way past the resplendent homes with the perfect landscapes. So many people yearned for these houses, she thought, but she didn't. She loved her tiny cottage and her world by the sea. She had no desire to live in an ant farm with these people.

As she came to a road on her right, she glanced down it and slowed. It looked like the construction site was on that cul de sac. A large cement truck was pulling out and several trucks were following it.

Maddy parked down the street making sure her car wouldn't be in the way of any other construction vehicles that would need to get through.

Tank spotted her first.

"I told you she'd be here," he said loudly enough for her to hear. Ryker slid off the tailgate of his truck where he had been sitting completing some paperwork. He tossed his clipboard into the bed and took the cooler from her. Tank hoisted the bag.

"How much stuff did you bring?" Tank asked, surprised at the weight.

"I know how much you guys can eat, and I didn't know if anyone else would need any food. There are a bunch of sandwiches there.

"That was thoughtful of you," Ryker said, "but the crew has left. They're going out to fix a roof issue at Cadigan's Marina now that the pour is done. The only one still here is Jaxx."

"Jaxx is here? I thought you wouldn't bring him on the job until you vetted him?" Maddy said, surprised. "But I have a sandwich for him, if he wants it."

"He came with some pretty impressive credentials. A few phone calls convinced me I wanted him on my team. Of course, I'm still making him jump through the hoops, just to be on the safe side, but I figured I might as well bring him out here where I could see him work with me."

As if Jaxx knew someone was talking about him, he turned his head their way. Recognizing Maddy, he smiled and gave her a lazy wave before he bent down to finish what he was doing.

"Come on over here, Jaxx. It's lunch break." Ryker reached into the back of his pickup and pulled out two camping chairs, unfolding them and offering one to Maddy. She plopped herself down in it and held out her hand to Tank, gesturing to him to give up the sandwich bag. She pointed to the cooler.

"Help yourselves to sodas. There are pepperoncini in there and sub sauce if you want it for your sandwich. Hi, Jaxx, have a sandwich." She smiled as the good-looking man walked up to her and she held out a wrapped sub. She didn't remember him looking this attractive last night, but she'd been in a mood. Today, his grin was very likable.

"Hi, Maddy. Thank you, but I'm sure you didn't plan on me being here for your picnic. I don't want to take someone else's food."

He declined the sandwich with an apologetic smile, embarrassed to be in the situation he found himself.

Tank enjoyed the man's discomfort. It was good to see this self-assured cowboy look out of sorts. Then Tank's thoughts changed. He just noticed the way Jaxx was looking at Maddy. Kind of hungry, but not for the sub.

Ryker noticed and shook his head slightly at his friend. Maddy was a big girl and could take care of herself.

Tank raised his eyebrows, a silent communication between them. He was thinking of the lonely drunk girl they took care of last night. Rebound is not what Maddy needed right now.

"Jaxx, please. I brought extra in case Ryker's crew was here and hungry, and it looked like I was right. Apparently, part of his crew is here. Are you hungry?" she asked, her face innocent and lit by the sun.

Tank almost growled out loud.

Jaxx grin turned a little predatory. At least Tank thought so. Maddy kind of thought it was sweet. She finished passing out the sandwiches and opened the bag of chips.

"I didn't bring plates. Sorry." she said, and she dug her hand in the bag, followed by Ryker and Tank. "We grew up together digging in bags. I didn't think about how someone else might feel." She said, suddenly embarrassed and she didn't know why.

"Honey, I was a Boy Scout. We camped for a week and forgot about washing our hands and we still dug into bags. Although, I have to admit, I've developed an affinity for soap and water as I've matured." He smiled good-naturedly and helped himself to a handful of the seasoned potato chips. "Damn, these are good."

"You've never had crab chips before?"

"They don't have those where I'm from," he said, enjoying the salty, spicy taste of the east coast seasoning.

"Where are you from?" Maddy asked as she took a bite of her sub.

"I lived most of my life in Colorado," he said. "Front Range, but I spent the last couple of years in Indiana working a large construction project."

"What brings you to Grey's Harbor?" Tank asked, keeping an eye on the interaction between the two.

"I worked with a guy who was from here. He talked fondly of the place. I'd never spent any time on the east coast, so I figured I might give it a try. There was nothing left for me back in Colorado, so I headed east." A shadow passed over his face for a moment, leaving him looking vulnerable, but it passed quickly.

"Maddy, he worked with Kenny Coleman. Remember he went to school for construction management and ended up with a huge construction company in the Midwest?"

"I haven't thought of Kenny for years. How's he doing?"

"Really well. He's married and has four kids with another on the way. I always admired how he was a happy guy who always treated people with dignity. When he said this was a great place, I figured if it produced a guy like Kenny, I should check it out. So, here I am."

"Well, welcome to Grey's Harbor. I think you'll like us," said Maddy kindly as she sipped her soda and contemplated the salami that was sliding from her bun. She missed the interesting look she was getting from Jaxx and the smoldering look Tank was giving him. Ryker just found the whole thing amusing. Tank always was the hot head of the bunch, ready to fight and ask questions later. Ryker also noticed that Jaxx was completely aware of the reaction he was getting from Tank. Jaxx dialed it back. He wasn't stupid, and he knew that he had a good thing here. He didn't want to make Tank worry. The guy was obviously protective of Maddy but didn't seem romantically involved.

Maddy finished her sandwich and hopped up from the chair.

"I hate to break up the party guys, but I have a lot of work to do. Ryker when do you plan on starting the window removal?"

"Whenever you're ready. Just say the word."

"I'm going to work in the studio today. I need to set up an area large enough to work on the windows. Do you think it will be a problem to do them one at a time?"

"No, I was going to suggest that. Yes, it means I have to run out there a lot, but it also means that I don't have to try to handle all the missing windows at once in Mirabelle's house. One boarded up window at a time is about all Mirabelle could handle, I would imagine."

"I should be ready by tomorrow, unless that's too early."

"Just call me tonight and we'll arrange a time. If you need help moving anything in your studio, just let me know, and thanks for the lunch, Maddy. It was awesome."

Tank and Jaxx nodded in agreement.

"Okay. I'm leaving the cooler and the sandwiches with you. Just bring the cooler back next time you see me. Bye guys." She gave Tank and Ryker a hug and awkwardly patted Jaxx's flannel clad arm, not sure what to do. He took her hand and thanked her again, dropping it in an appropriate amount of time. Even Tank couldn't find fault with the gesture

9

*M*addy rang the antique bell on the front door of Miss Mirabelle's home, again admiring the monogramed glass panel despite her distaste for the situation she was finding herself in. She was excited to work on the exquisite windows, but she didn't want to deal with the woman anymore. The lawyer had shut the door on any kind feelings Maddy may have had.

The door opened and Ryker bowed, bidding her to enter.

"You're an ass," she said, slapping him lightly on the arm.

"True, but I'm the kind of ass who you thank later." He grinned at her in his easy way, but she knew him well. She was about to be set up.

"What are you up to? Is Mirabelle lurking around and you're excited to watch me squirm?"

"Nope. She said the noise was going to put her off, so she called her driver to take her and Miss Maggie to town."

"What the hell are Miss Mirabelle and Miss Maggie going to do in town? What does an old woman and standard poodle do in town?" she repeated, shaking her head.

"Whatever the rich lady and her pampered pooch care to do," a disembodied voice said from the front parlor.

"Who's that?" asked Maddy, suddenly concerned for the windows when she heard the squeal of a nail pulling out of wood.

"Jaxx," said Ryker easily with a grin on his face.

"What's gotten into you?" Maddy said, perplexed.

"Not a damn thing. Come on, tell us how you want this window packed."

Maddy followed Ryker into the front parlor where Jaxx was removing the last of the moulding from the window. He was meticulous, the process painstakingly slow.

"I think I've got the last of it. Just one more nail and it'll be free. None of the moulding split, which is some kind of miracle. Hey, Maddy. Window remover extraordinaire at your service," Jaxx said, his cocky confidence evident in his self-assured grin.

"Ryker, I thought you and Tank were going to do this," she said nervously, suddenly concerned about what she was getting into.

"Tank begged off. He felt the same way you do about combining his brawn and Mirabelle's delicate windows. Jaxx said he was used to delicate operations, so I thought I'd give him a shot."

"Kinda a risky way to vet someone, don't you think?" she asked dryly.

"I figured you can fix anything we break, right?" Ryker teased.

Jaxx snorted at the look on Maddy's face.

"Maybe it would be better if you left and we brought this to you without you having to watch," Jaxx suggested.

"Not necessarily a bad plan." Ryker agreed.

"Trust me, Maddy. I know what I'm doing. I'll deliver this window to you with no further damage than what Mother Nature did."

"My friend, I don't trust anyone I just met. No offense," Maddy said, not entirely kidding.

"Smart girl. I approve, but believe me, before this is over, you will trust me with your life." He stopped what he was doing and looked at her intently.

Within seconds Maddy's world changed. Electricity shot through her with his words, leaving her tingling and slightly short of breath. What the hell had just happened? Jaxx's eyes were smoldering, and he was obviously enjoying her discomfort. She stared at him, her lips parted, her mind wondering what he looked like under that flannel shirt. She swallowed hard, trying to snap out of it. She tore her eyes from Jaxx and glanced at Ryker. He just shrugged and grinned, clearly amused.

She was off balance, confused, and Jaxx took pity on her. He softened his eyes and his voice, soothing her with a glance. Controlling her skillfully, which just unnerved her even more.

"Look, Maddy. I know you don't trust me...yet. It's okay, but I did some restoration work on a building in Chicago. Granted, I didn't remove stained glass like this, but I worked with some delicate woodwork and glass fixtures. Same idea, different material. Have faith." He smiled so the corners of his eyes crinkled, and she immediately felt calm. She watched him for a minute, holding his eyes, then made a decision that felt right.

"Okay. I'm going back to the studio. You guys bring that over when it's ready, and thank you for being careful," she added for good measure.

"I'll walk you out, Maddy. Be back in a minute, Jaxx." Ryker put his hand on the small of Maddy's back and led her out the big front doors.

"What do you know about that guy, Ryker?" Maddy asked, suddenly concerned now that she was out of Jaxx influence.

"Enough to feel good about him. He served this country with distinction, and he was granted a Purple Heart. I know there's a lot more, but it's his story to tell, not mine. He doesn't know that I know about this, and I'm going to keep it that way until he decides to share, if he ever decides to. Fair enough?" he asked her.

"Fair enough," she agreed, her mind wandering to the man inside wondering where the scar was that earned him that medal.

"We'll be by the studio soon. See you then." Ryker opened the car door for Maddy and gave her a hug before she crawled in. "And Maddy. I know you're a tough girl and all, but I also know you're hurt. I don't know if you remember, but you spilled your guts to us the other night. Not just about Tripp, but about what Miss Mirabelle told you. It's okay to be hurt, but don't let it define you. Okay?" He tilted her chin, forcing her to look at him. Jaxx watched from the window. He imagined his fingers on her soft skin.

"Okay, Ryker. I hear you. And thanks for listening the other night. I remember. I just didn't want to talk about it anymore."

"I figured. You weren't that drunk," he said with a smile.

Maddy's gaze moved toward the house. She felt more than saw Jaxx in the window as he continued to work, but somehow, she knew he was watching her. He was dangerous, she decided. He could be very dangerous for her, and she was determined that he not wound her in the process.

10

*B*ack at her studio, Maddy looked around trying to decide how to best use the space. Her regular cutting table was an old partners' desk, heavy and square, the surface not big enough to handle the windows. What she needed was something wide and long like a dining room table. She considered moving the table in from the house but dismissed the idea immediately. She didn't need to be eating off a surface where she had worked with lead. Not a good plan. She tapped her finger on the partners' desk, willing it to be somehow bigger when her eyes fell on the Dutch doors. A door would be perfect. A plan in mind, she went into the house and down into the basement. Within minutes she was heading back up the stairs, an old flat door removed from its hinges clasped in her hands as she struggled up to the first floor.

"Maddy, are you in there?" Ryker's voice rang out as he called through the back screen door.

"Down here," she answered. "Come in, and I need help, please," her voice strained with the struggle.

Ryker and Jaxx looked at each other, both registering the word help at the same time, and they jockeyed for position as they both tried to squeeze through the door together. Jaxx made it first as he burst into the cottage.

His training kicked into gear as he quickly assessed that the room he entered seemed empty. Ryker, right behind him, didn't want to laugh. He knew he was watching a vet switch into combat mode, but he also knew Maddy's voice, and she wasn't in trouble, just in a predicament.

"Maddy, where are you? Are you hurt?" Jaxx voice was stern and commanding. Demanding an answer.

Maddy giggled despite herself.

"I'm on the basement stairs, and I'm fine. I just need a hand."

Jaxx turned toward the voice and spotted the open door and the stairs leading down. He crossed the room quickly glancing around, gathering information. When he caught sight of her, he pulled up short.

"What are you doing?" he asked as he took in the scene, the slight girl struggling with the large, heavy door.

"Bringing this door upstairs, what does it look like I'm doing?"

Jaxx shook his head and reached down the stairs relieving Maddy of the burden. She shook out her arms and thanked him sweetly.

Jaxx breathed allowing the adrenaline to dissipate. It wasn't necessary that he had gone into full defense, but he couldn't help himself. His body remembered, and it betrayed him. *Breathe*, he thought. *Breathe*.

Maddy watched him, knowing he had an internal struggle, but not completely understanding it. More than anything she wanted him to be comfortable, but she didn't know how to respond.

She waited, pretending to rub the muscles in her arms as if they were overtaxed.

"Okay, where do you want this and why are we doing this?" Jaxx asked casually, trying to cover his anxiety. He juggled the door, making the turn, careful not to hit anything as he moved the awkward piece of wood through the doorway. At that moment the sun moved from behind a cloud and beams of light filled the windows, lighting up the colored glass panels that hung in front of them. The sight instantly calmed him.

"Wow," he said. "That's beautiful." The tough guy act disappeared. "Maddy, did you do all of these?"

She nodded, suddenly shy of her work. He leaned the door against the wall and walked over to a tall narrow stained-glass panel. Seeded clear glass filled the background as a single iris captured the center, it's impossibly narrow stem gracefully curving its way from the leaves to the flower.

"That piece of glass, that stem, had to be really hard to cut and without breaking the stem in half. It's amazing." He looked at the delicate mix of petals in various shades of lavender, the soft folds replicating nature, the stamen cut of tiny pieces of yellow glass coming alive with light.

He glanced at her hands expecting to see cuts and scars, but there weren't any. She understood his look.

"Oh, believe me, I've been cut many, many times. I've just been on a lucky streak." She grinned and knocked on a wooden Boston rocker that stood in front of the fireplace. "Don't want to tempt fate."

"Okay, so where are we taking this door?" Jaxx asked, taking control again of the situation.

"Let me guess," Ryker piped up. "You're taking it to the studio to make a table big enough to hold the windows, and you don't care right now that it's going to be destroyed."

"Exactly. I'm going to put it on top of the partners' desk, but I've just got to figure out how to fix it so it doesn't slide around. My studio is going to feel a whole lot smaller," she said as she looked at the door again. It looked huge. Maybe the idea wasn't such a hot one.

Jaxx picked up the door again and followed Ryker and Maddy out onto the porch and down the shell path to the studio.

"This place is incredible," said Jaxx as he stopped for a minute to stare over the beach and out across the ocean. "I could sit here forever and never get bored of watching the water."

Maddy looked at the man. She could see pain in his face that was looking for an escape. He watched the ocean hungrily like he was waiting for it to wash something away, something that was eating him. In a second it was gone and replaced with a smile.

"Thanks. I love it, too. I don't think I could ever leave here and feel like I was at home somewhere else." This time it was her turn as her face stiffened with the memory of Tripp asking her to come with him, to leave her home.

Jaxx didn't miss a trick. He also didn't like that look on her face. He wanted to protect her from that pain, but he didn't know what it was. Suddenly, it became his job to figure it out and eliminate whatever threat was there.

"And Jaxx, you're welcome any time to come out here and just sit. There are plenty of chairs on the back porch, and that path takes you through the dunes to the beach. Anytime," she repeated.

Maddy opened the bottom of the Dutch door and Jaxx and Ryker stepped in, flipping the door on top of the partner's desk. Ryker studied the situation and told them he'd be right back.

"He's probably going to get some clamps so this won't slide around," Jaxx said, checking out the edge of the desk to see if clamps were going to work. Maddy walked around the door table, imagining working on the windows, wondering if she was going to have enough room to do everything she needed to.

When Jaxx was satisfied, he wandered around the studio looking at the glass panels that hung from the rafters and the bowls that graced the shelves. Then he glanced into the open kiln seeing the bowl blanks, stacked pieces of glass waiting to be fused. He glanced back at the finished bowls and realization dawned on him.

"Stained glass only melted together and then melted into a mold?" he asked, studying the computer controller on the kiln.

"Essentially," she responded, looking critically at the assembled blanks. "I have a few more to finish for a pending order, then I can concentrate on the windows. I'm just not going to have enough room to do both."

She sucked her lower lip between her teeth, trying to puzzle out what she needed to do. Jaxx watched her brow furrow. He wanted to smooth it. Fix the problem, but he wasn't sure what it was.

Suddenly Maddy smiled, and the world lit up. He felt himself relax and smile with her. He didn't know what just changed, but he liked it.

"What?" he asked.

"I've got work to do. You have the window in the truck, right?"

"Yeah, you want me to bring it in?" Jaxx asked, wanting to do it for her, but knowing he had to wait for Ryker to handle the big piece so it wouldn't break.

"No, not yet. I have to do something quickly before you guys do that. Do you think you have time, is Ryker in a hurry?"

"Ryker is not in a hurry."

They both turned to see Ryker coming through the door, his hands full of clamps. Within minutes, Ryker and Jaxx had the door clamped down.

"Will that work?' Jaxx asked, concerned. He looked at all the clamps Maddy would have to work around.

"Let's find out," she said.

Ryker and Jaxx watched as she walked over to a large wooden rack that held sheets of glass. Sliding a pair of safety glasses onto her face, she pulled out a clear sheet that measured nearly two feet by three feet. Handling it carefully, she carried it over to the newly designed table and laid it down gently. Jaxx marveled her hands weren't already cut from the sharp edges. She consulted a piece of paper and pulled the large circle cutter off the shelf. Measuring out the size she needed, she expertly scribed the first large circle on the left hand side of the glass. Then she scribed a second one right next to it. Checking her notes again, she adjusted the circle cutter and cut four more small blanks, fitting them in here and there like a baker trying to get the last cookie cut out of the scraps of dough.

When there was no more room for any other circles, Maddy made a few quick relief cuts and then used her running pliers to control the breaks. In seconds, perfect circles were freed from the glass and the scraps were moved to the scrap bin. She crossed the studio and repeated the procedure three more times.

Jaxx marveled at the cool assurance with which she handled the glass, her fingers flying, never faltering or hesitating. He realized he was watching a master at work. He also realized she had forgotten they were there. Her concentration was on the glass. There was nothing but the glass and the sound of the cutters as they broke the surface tension.

When she was finished, she looked up triumphantly.

"I have all the blanks I need to cut from the large sheets, so I can finish the bowl order. The details I'll cut from smaller pieces, so I won't need a big space. I won't have a large enough area once the window is on the table. Luckily the breaks in the window are in smaller areas of glass, so I should be okay. If I have to cut a big sheet, I'll just have to get creative, or just take it into the house and cut in on the dining room table." She thought about it but imagined stepping on a stray glass shard with her bare feet. She didn't like that idea, so she was going to try to avoid it.

"Are you ready for us to bring the window in?" Ryker asked.

"As ready as I'm ever going to be," Maddy said, grinning with anticipation.

*O*nce the window was unpacked and carefully laid on Maddy's new work surface, Maddy began to feel the excitement build within her. She was going to get to work on a piece of history. *Her history* a voice in her head reminded her. *No, not my history, Mirabelle's,* her inner voice hissed.

She studied the glass, running her hands over the lead cames, inspecting the ancient putty that held the colored glass in place. What these windows had seen, the families who had grown up with them, the children who gazed through them or watched the colors as they moved up the walls, keeping with the sun's travels. Maddy was mesmerized, pulled into them as she considered how she was going to start, what pieces were going to get her first attention.

Jaxx watched her. He saw her draw inward, concentrate on the task at hand. He remembered that feeling. Zoning in, his concentration a pinpoint. Listen and feel for the enemy. Watch the target. Keep his men safe.

He saw a slow smile spread across Maddy's face. She didn't even remember they were there. She was an artist coming to terms with the piece she was going to touch, and she was beautiful in the moment.

Ryker cleared his throat, breaking the spell for both of them.

"So, you good? Is this where you need it so you can work? Will you need to pick it up, shift it?" He looked anxious.

"Nope, at least not for a while. Thanks Ryker, I've got it from here." She smiled at him reassuring him that all was well. "And Jaxx, I was serious about the beach. You can come anytime."

"Thanks. Maybe I'll take you up on it. I'd like that."

Ryker rolled his eyes. As tough as Jaxx was, a soldier, a purple-heart recipient, he seemed like he was afraid of a mere girl. *Make a date, already*, Ryker thought.

Jaxx just smiled at him, cocky. *Playing it cool, man,* he telegraphed.

Ryker just snorted at him. On the way out the door, Ryker snagged one of Maddy's business cards off a holder on the windowsill. He handed it to Jaxx as they walked the shell path back to the truck.

"Here's her number. Just give her a call. She doesn't bite."

"Hmm," Jaxx said, as he slid the card in the front chest pocket of his flannel shirt. He just might do that. He could see himself sitting next to Maddy Grey on that back porch, his feet on the rail and doing nothing but watching the ocean pull his thoughts out to sea.

The phone startled Maddy. She had been working steadily for hours, removing pieces of broken glass and tracing new patterns. She had just been about to start pulling some sample glass to make sure she had a good match when she was interrupted.

She sighed and looked at the phone screen. It was a number she didn't recognize, but that didn't mean she wouldn't answer. In this business, she didn't know where the next job would come from. All calls were answered or returned.

"Hello, this is Maddy Grey. How can I help you?"

"Do you like pepperoni, sausage, and onion pizza?"

"Excuse me?" Maddy asked, irritated her work was interrupted for a prank.

"If you don't like pizza, I could probably eat it all myself, but you did say I could stop by and watch the ocean from your place. I didn't think it was right coming empty handed."

"Jaxx!" Maddy smiled feeling the irritation melt away. "I adore pepperoni pizza, and onions and sausage are acceptable additions." Her stomach growled at the thought. "I hope it's a big one, and I am assuming you've discovered Harbor New York?"

"Ryker steered me in the correct direction for pizza. I'm picking it up now. Is there anything else you need or want?"

"I have some beer and soda in the fridge if that works for you."

"It does. I'll be there in a few." The phone went dead and Maddy stood in her studio trying to decide how she felt. The smile plastered on her face should have been a clue, but her heart was thinking of Tripp. She looked at the watercolor again, a painful reminder of what happens when you let someone into your life.

Her phone rang again.

"Hello, Jaxx. What's wrong?"

"I forgot to ask; how do you feel about dogs?"

"You mean a hundred and fifty pound bull mastiff named Betty?"

"That would be the one."

"I'd love to meet her...I think."

Maddy slid the phone into her pocket and looked around the studio. It was later than she realized, the sun moving low in the sky. It was her favorite time of evening when everything slowed down and the beach was lit with a rosy glow. She quickly cleaned up her area and turned off the lights. Enough for tonight.

Inside the cottage, Maddy washed her hands thoroughly, making sure all the lead remains were cleaned from her skin. She scrubbed her face and pulled the ponytail from her hair, brushing the long dark tresses. She stared at herself in the mirror. *No, not like that.* She wasn't doing it like that this evening. She gathered her mane into her hands and secured the ponytail back where it belonged. She wanted to be Maddy. Just Maddy and no one else.

*J*axx found her sitting on the back deck in a metal tulip chair with a small cooler at her feet. He watched her from the corner of the house. She hadn't seen him yet. He studied her, the tilt of her head, the line of her jaw; it was strong and independent. He couldn't see her eyes, but he knew they were sad. He could feel the sadness, could see it in her shoulders. She had been hurt, badly. Not a gunshot wound, like Greg. Not the gaping hole that shot blood five feet away, but pain just the same. Greg was surprised when he was hit. It showed on his face. Just an 'oops, that wasn't supposed to happen' and then nothing. For Greg the pain was gone. It hadn't lasted. His buddies picked it up for him. Let it live in them for an eternity. Jaxx knew about pain. The pain from shrapnel and bullets cut deep. It hurt for a long time, but there were other kinds of pain that cut deeper and never went away. Maddy had that kind of pain.

It made him mad.

He was trained to handle that. It was drilled into him that people died. People left you. Your buddies would die, but you never left them. You never ever left your friends. And you carried their pain.

Betty whimpered softly from where she sat at his side. She licked Jaxx's hand making certain he was present. He was. She looked where he was looking. At the girl. The sad girl on the porch. Betty knew how to handle sad girls on porches.

She looked up at Jaxx and whimpered again, softly.

"Go," he whispered.

Betty kicked up sand as she raced around the back of the porch and bounded up the steps full on love machine waiting to introduce herself to Maddy.

Maddy startled as she saw the massive, musclebound canine rushing toward her. She braced herself for the onslaught knowing she couldn't outrun the dog. She gripped the arms of the chair looking around wildly for Jaxx, fully aware that this had to be his dog.

No time left, the dog was nearly upon her when Jaxx spoke.

"Betty, sit."

And Betty skidded into sit, directly in front of the hyperventilating Maddy.

"Betty, say hello."

Betty primly offered her paw.

"Maddy, say hello back," Jaxx commanded.

Maddy shook herself and laughed, grateful she hadn't peed herself right then and there.

"Hello, Betty. Pleased to make your acquaintance."

The dog looked delighted at the formality.

Jaxx waited at the steps, the big pizza box in his hands.

"Come on up and bring that box with you. I'm starved." She gestured to the white wicker table that was pushed up against the house, a beautiful folded glass vase holding a bouquet of sunflowers plopped in the center. Paper plates and napkins sat next to the vase with a shaker of pepper flakes and a shaker of cheese.

"Well, good. You know how to eat pizza," he said, gesturing to the pepper flakes.

She just grinned and reached over to lift the lid of the box Jaxx had placed on the table. *Damn that smelled amazing*, she thought.

"I can't get over how good that pizza smells," Jaxx said. "I hope it tastes just as good."

"Oh, I can assure you, it tastes even better."

As the sun rode low in the sky, washing the ocean with the pastels of dusk, Maddy and Jaxx ate pizza and shared the 'bones' with Betty.

Maddy finished her second piece, then slid her eyes toward Jaxx, watching him. He was polishing off a slice, taking a bite of the remaining crust. She could see the indecision. He wanted to eat the rest of the buttery, garlicky, crisp tender edge, but Betty was staring at him intently. She was too well trained and too polite to beg, a woof would be totally unacceptable, but turning those liquid brown eyes on her master was fair game.

Jaxx grinned at his dog.

"You win," he told her as he tossed the pizza bone to her. She caught it expertly. Maddy expected her to swallow it whole. After all, she was a huge dog and the piece of crust wasn't large.

She didn't. The giant dog lifted her muzzle to the sky, closed her eyes, and chewed the crust with such reverence Maddy couldn't help but burst out laughing. When the dog was done, she turned those eyes on Maddy, the hurt in them unmistakable.

"Oh no, Betty. I'm sorry I laughed at you. Come here, girl." Maddy patted her thighs encouraging the dog to come over.

"Wait," Jaxx said, but it was too late. The massive dog understood that gesture. That was the 'it's okay to come up on my lap' gesture. And she did. All one hundred and fifty pounds of dog made themselves at home on Maddy's tiny lap, pizza plate and all.

And then the dog washed Maddy's face thoroughly. After all, Maddy had asked for some love.

Jaxx sprang out of the chair and hauled Betty off Maddy admonishing the dog to go lay down. Betty did, looking confused and miserable, her considerable tail tucked between her legs.

"Maddy, I'm sorry. Are you okay?" Jaxx crouched in front of her chair, his eyes level with hers.

Maddy wiped her face with a napkin and came up grinning.

"I'm fine, Jaxx. Really, I am. That's one big dog."

"Seriously, Maddy. Did she hurt you?" He reached out and lifted her chin, forcing her eyes to his. He was assessing her. Looking for the lies everyone told to hide hurt. The same ones he told. But he was an expert on reading people. He was trained to find the weakness.

Maddy stared back at him. She knew she was being examined. Normally it would have made her squirm. She didn't want just anyone close. Only her tiny circle of friends. And Tripp. There was, of course, Tripp. She let him in, and it was a mistake. He hurt her, and it was a different hurt than her thighs were feeling right now. Tripp hurt was deep and forever.

Jaxx's eyes went from earnest searching to a hard glint. He'd found it. He perceived the shift instantly.

"What's hurting you, Maddy?" he asked, quietly. He knew he could interrogate her. Break her. He also knew he mustn't. She wasn't the enemy. She was the victim. The enemy remained to be seen.

"I'm fine," she repeated again, a wall closing the communication between them, her eyes hooded. "She didn't even scratch me, and look, now her feelings are hurt even more." She broke away from his intense examination and glanced at the sulking dog.

Jaxx's eyes slid to Betty.

Her tail thumped against the wooden porch floor. They were good. Solid.

He turned his attention back to Maddy.

"Okay, but what else hurts?" he asked, waiting.

"Nothing." She whispered, once again caught up in his eyes.

"Nothing that you care to tell me," he told her.

Her cheeks colored slightly.

He knew when to back down. He knew he could get what he wanted from her any time. He could bully her into telling him who hurt her, but that would destroy the mission, compromise the relationship. He was startled to discover that he was interested in strengthening this relationship. It had been a long time.

"So, what hurts you?" Maddy asked, her eyebrow cocked.

She didn't miss a trick either.

Jaxx slid his mouth into a cold half grin, a trick his buddies would have recognized. They had seen it after Justine and Kaelie's death. A signal that they needed to back off, and that he was trying to move away from the memory. A signal they always respected.

A signal that Betty never missed.

The dog stood up and walked to Jaxx side and leaned against him. A strong, calm presence.

"What hurts me," he answered, his emotions locked, "is a pizza getting cold."

He stood and handed her a clean plate.

Maddy was smart. She knew to move past this moment, but she also knew it wasn't finished, for either of them.

They both helped themselves to another piece and settled into a comfortable silence, eating top notch pizza and letting the ocean waves pull at their souls.

"Jaxx?" Maddy said, a half hour of silence later.

"Hmmm?" he asked, comfortably sated.

"You know how those waves come in strong and pull back out?"

"Yep."

"They clean the beach, Jaxx. Sometimes they bring up a lot of bad stuff, but in the end, they always manage to clean the beach."

"I can see that."

"You're welcome anytime on my porch when your beach needs cleaning."

She didn't look at him. His peripheral vision was studying her. She never looked at him.

He respected that.

12

*M*addy checked the window meticulously making sure all of the putty was cleaned from the glass. The repair went much easier than she expected. She knew better than to think that all the windows would be this easy, but she was hopeful. The windows had been very well made and obviously cared for over the years. If they were all like this, she would make a tidy profit on a job that wouldn't take as long as she anticipated. She thought about the other glass in Mirabelle's house. She wondered when a good time would be to broach the subject of extending her contract to include some interior work. She knew it was too early for that, but the time would come, she was sure of it, although she didn't relish dealing with Mirabelle or her rude attorney, and she didn't want another creepy conversation about her heritage. It just didn't matter to her. Whatever her ancestors did, or who they did, just wasn't important to her. She was Maddy. The Grey was incidental. Just Maddy and that was that.

She picked up the phone and called Ryker.

"Hey, Maddy? How's it going?"

"Good Ryker. In fact, I have this window done, so it's ready whenever you are to take it back and install it."

"That means you need another window, too."

"Bingo. You're a bright man, my friend, unless it comes to women, then you are a total loser."

"Wow, Maddy. You don't pull any punches. What do you have against Margot?"

"Oh, Ryker. There are some lessons you need to learn all by yourself."

"Who's Margot?"

"Jaxx? Is that you?"

"Yeah, it's Jaxx," said Ryker. "I have you on speaker phone. Sorry, I should have warned you."

"No worries. You guys sound busy. Just let me know when you want to make the switch and install this window. I'd like to be there for that process."

"You mean you'd like to micromanage us," Ryker corrected.

"Perhaps," Maddy said sweetly as she bid them a good day and cleared the phone call.

Satisfied that the window was ready, she pulled a couple of bowl blanks off the shelf and set to cleaning them. She needed to get the last bowls in the kiln so she could finish up this order. She was beginning to feel the pressure of the deadline.

Maddy worked steadily all morning, windows open, the sound of the waves soothing her soul and stoking her creativity. Blues and greens captured the ocean's spirit in her bowls, transforming plain pieces of glass into stunning works of art.

She never heard Ryker and Jaxx approach the studio. Ryker started up to the door, but Jaxx put his hand on Ryker's arm stopping him. He wanted to watch her work. He could see her profile, catching occasional glimpses of her face. He was surprised to see it looking free and relaxed, totally different from the other times he'd studied her. She was in her element, her soul free as she created. He felt a tug in his heart, a tiny crack in the armored surface. He knew he wanted to get to know this remarkable woman, to know her in every way there was to know her, but he wasn't ready. And neither was she.

Ryker watched Jaxx. He hadn't known this man very long, but he trusted him. Ryker had pretty good instincts when it came to men. His sister and Maddy kept telling him he sucked at judging women, but they were a different species. A man couldn't be blamed for screwing up there, but he was fairly certain about Jaxx. This man was straight up, and Ryker knew that he would protect Maddy. Ryker's heart had broken for her when Tripp left. Maddy was always pretty reserved, an introvert. Losing Tripp had just turned her even more inward, even more reclusive. It wasn't good. Not for someone so full of life and wisdom as Maddy. Ryker had a feeling these two would be really good for each other. They both had some baggage that needed tossed, and he hoped that they could do it for each other.

"This isn't safe," Jaxx said suddenly.

"What?" said Ryker, looking around for what he may have missed.

"She doesn't even have a clue we're out here. She's isolated. Her situational awareness sucks. She should have a sense we're watching her."

Suddenly, Maddy stiffened. She looked up from her work, her creative spell broken, and she looked around carefully.

Through the open top of the Dutch door she caught sight of Ryker and Jaxx and her face broke into a wide smile. It made Jaxx heart crack just a little more.

"How long have you guys been standing there watching me?" she asked, surprised at how happy she was to see Jaxx.

"Long enough to know that you aren't safe out here," Jaxx growled.

"Oh shit. Now you did it," Ryker said, taking a retreating step.

The smile stilled on Maddy's face. It wasn't the first time she had heard this, but she wasn't going to take it from this guy who just came into her life, who didn't even really know her.

"I am perfectly fine here, safe here by myself. I've lived here for years, and I'm perfectly capable of taking care of myself, thank you very much. Are you here to lecture me or to do your job and pick up this window?" she said, a severe frost in her voice.

"A little of both," Jaxx said, rising to the occasion. He wasn't the least bit intimidated by this diminutive fireball. He had faced much larger explosions in his time.

"Well, my safety is none of your business."

Ryker smiled and took a load off, settling into a small bench outside the studio. It seemed like a really good time to contemplate the ocean.

"Well, darlin', we were watching you for a good three minutes before you even noticed. If I wanted to, I could have been up behind you before you would have reacted. You had no early warning, no knowledge you might have been in danger. That is unacceptable."

"Unacceptable to whom?"

"To me, that's whom."

"Who."

"What?"

"Who not whom. It's not whom in this instance."

"Your superior command of the English language is not pertinent currently. Your safety and well-being are. Do you work here at night, in the dark, with no blinds on these windows?" he asked, stalking around, his practiced eye looking at the studio for the first time as a security risk.

"I work whenever my little heart desires," she said sweetly with a dangerous undertone running through her words. "No one is here to tell me what to do or not to do." She took a deep breath. "And I like it like that." It may not have been true, but it worked for her right now.

They stared each other down, neither flinching.

Ryker started whistling a low, tuneless song. He waited. The first one to speak loses. He knew that, and apparently so did the both of them.

The silence stretched on.

"Hello, Madeline?" a voice called out.

Ryker stood up from the bench.

"Hello, Miss Mirabelle. What brings you out this way?" asked Ryker, giving Maddy and Jaxx a minute to collect themselves.

"Why my windows, of course." She looked at him, and he felt himself dismissed. It wasn't that she was mean, it was just her way, her training. He knew she really couldn't help herself, and he didn't take offense. Ryker was too easy going for that. Maddy and Jaxx, on the other hand, were not cut from the same cloth.

Jaxx broke the stare first. He had the impression Maddy would have kept going had he not glanced away. Maddy wasn't going to demure to Miss Mirabelle.

Now this was interesting, he thought to himself. *I like that backbone she's got.*

Mirabelle pushed the lower door open, allowing herself access to the studio. She glanced around, taking in the glittering world, then her gaze settled on Maddy and Jaxx. Despite her age, she was still astute at reading people and sexual tension, and it was thick as thieves in here.

"I've come to see how you're doing on my windows," Mirabelle announced to Maddy.

"Hello, Miss Mirabelle. I really wish you would have called first. My studio isn't open to visitors. I don't have insurance for the public to be in my studio."

"I am hardly public, my dear," she said. "I'm family."

"Seriously, I'm not interested in rehashing this. We are not by any stretch of the imagination family."

Jaxx, sensing her distress, moved closer. He wanted to caution her to be careful. He had already figured out that Miss Mirabelle was an important and formidable entity in this town that carried her last name. Maddy didn't seem to care.

"Yes, you are, Madeline, and you're going to have to face that fact one of these days."

"I don't have to do anything of the sort. I will remind you that my name is Maddy, and I have a job to do. That job is to fix your windows. We have an agreement. But that's where this relationship ends. We're not tied in any way. Not at all."

"Come here, my dear." Miss Mirabelle gestured for Maddy to join her as she moved toward a window.

Maddy sighed in exasperation but did what she was told.

"What, Miss Mirabelle?" she asked as Jaxx came up beside her.

"Do you see that old foundation over there, the ruins?"

"Of course. They've been there all my life. Nothing new there, Miss Mirabelle."

"Do you know what foundations those are? Rather whose."

"No, Miss Mirabelle, I don't, but I'm sure you're going to tell me." Maddy's head was beginning to hurt. Jaxx wanted to reach out and smooth the tension in her brow, but he didn't. He glanced at Ryker as he made is way over to stand next the two of them, a united front.

"Once there was a cottage here, a lot like yours, but it was claimed by the sea in a hurricane. Your namesake lived there, Madeline Abuchon. This was her place. Her property."

Mirabelle smiled, enjoying the stunned look on Maddy's face. It was enough for today, she decided. She walked over to the repaired window and gave it a cursory glance.

"The window looks lovely, my dear. Ryker, is it going to be installed soon?"

"Yes, ma'am. Maybe this afternoon, and we'll be removing the next window if that fits your schedule."

"Of course, Ryker. Whatever you need to do. You know I trust your judgement." She smiled at the man. She always liked Ryker Winn and his sister, Maeve. It's too bad he was involved with that socialite Margot Kennedy. He could do better.

She nodded her goodbyes to Maddy and the man, *what was his name? Jaxx. Strange name.*

"Let me walk you to your car, Miss Mirabelle," Ryker offered. It had been a rough half hour in that studio, and he wanted to give Maddy and Jaxx a few minutes to sort out just where they stood now.

Maddy scrubbed her face with her hands, exasperation oozing from her pores. Jaxx took her hands gently in his and pulled them carefully from her face.

"Truce?" he asked.

"Please," she nodded, suddenly wanting to bury her head into his shoulder, willing him to wrap his arms around her.

Jaxx knew people.

He obliged.

13

*R*yker stopped short, watching the two of them embrace, Jaxx tenderly holding Maddy, her shoulders slumped in defeat. Jaxx glanced at him, daring him to say something. Ryker just nodded at him, then made some noise as he came through the door.

"Hey Maddy, did you want to come with us to install this thing, or have you had enough of the old bat today?"

That brought a smile to her lips as she pulled away from Jaxx, feeling a little self-conscious. She considered her options.

"Don't let her win," Jaxx suggested, resisting the urge to put his arm around her.

"You're right. I won't let her win. Even though the woman wears me down something terrible, she isn't going to beat me. I don't care what she has to say, it doesn't have anything to do with me."

"That's my girl," said Ryker. "And when we're done installing the window, how about we head to the Mizzen Mast. I could use an Izzy fish fry. Anyone else?"

"That's right, it's Friday. What about Margot?" Maddy asked.

"It's Friday. Friday is for family. I'm not family," Ryker said wryly.

"Okay, I'm in," said Maddy with a smile.

"I remember Izzy," Jaxx said, "Tough looking lady who I wouldn't want to cross?"

Ryker and Maddy nodded.

"Okay, I'm in," said Jaxx.

Ryker and Jaxx readied the window in the packing Maddy had saved then carried it out to the truck while Maddy closed up the studio. Jaxx met her at the door as she locked it securely.

"Hey, Maddy. I'm sorry I came on a little strong earlier. Occupational hazard."

"No problem. I understand where you're coming from, and I appreciate your concern, but this is Grey's Harbor, and I'm safe here, even out here on the isolated beach. Trust me," she said, earnestly looking up into his eyes.

"Okay, for now, but I'd still like to talk with you about a few things just to give me peace of mind. Is that fair?" He asked.

She considered his words.

"I suppose, but not now. Is that fair?"

"Absolutely. And maybe, if you feel like talking, you can fill me in on whatever Miss Mirabelle thinks she has that she can hold over your head, because I have the feeling that this isn't over yet."

"Yeah, I have the same feeling. She's playing some kind of silly game, and I have no idea why."

*W*hen they got to Mirabelle's place, she was nowhere to be found. Ryker had a key because of his ongoing contract work with her, so after a polite knock, he let them in. Maddy couldn't watch as they installed the window. It made her nervous, so she wandered around looking at the stained-glass transoms over the doors in the house, noting which ones needed maintenance work. When she was done, she meandered back to where Ryker and Jaxx were putting the last of the moulding around the window.

"Maddy, is it okay if we remove the next window tomorrow morning and bring it by then? I promise it'll be bright and early, but I just got an alert that we have a storm rolling in tonight and I would rather do it after that passes. I have all the damaged windows protected, and I would like to leave them that way tonight."

"No worries. That makes sense. I wouldn't have been doing any work on it tonight anyway. Are you done here?"

"Yep, let's get some fish. You guys want to ride with me over to Izzy's?"

"Sure," said Jaxx. "Just drop me at my truck when we're done. It's still at your shop."

"Can do, but you really need to get that starter looked at," Ryker teased.

"I know, but I'm new in town. I don't have a trusted mechanic yet," said Jaxx as they walked out the front door and Ryker carefully locked up the house.

"Holden Roberts at Stevenson Auto Repair," Ryker and Maddy said in unison, then both started laughing.

"Apparently he's the man?"

"Best mechanic in town and an all-around nice guy," said Maddy as they walked to Ryker's truck. "And if you need a vehicle while yours is in the garage, just let me know. You can use mine. I can easily work around not having a car for a couple of days."

She smiled at him as he started to protest.

Ryker opened the door for Maddy to slide in the truck.

"Get used to it, Jaxx," he said. "The people in Grey's Harbor take care of each other."

⚓

The Mizzen Mast was hopping when they got there. Izzy was behind the bar and she nodded to the three of them as they made their way to a corner table. As they got settled, Izzy wiped her hands on a towel and came over.

"What are you drinking tonight?" she asked, looking with interest at Maddy and Jaxx. There was something brewing there.

Ryker met her eyes and nodded.

"Maddy, the usual?" he asked.

"Sure," she said as she stretched, working some kinks out of her back.

"What's the usual?" Jaxx asked, looking up at Izzy.

"Sperm Whale Ale," she told him her lips quirking up in a smile.

"What the hell?" he asked,

"Just go with it," Maddy told him. "You lived in Colorado where they eat Rocky Mountain Oysters. Don't judge."

"Good point," he replied. "Make it three."

Izzy nodded.

"Fish fry?" she asked.

"Yes ma'am," Ryker said.

"Onion rings instead of fries for you two, how about you, Jaxx?" Izzy asked, looking coolly into his eyes. He had the uncomfortable feeling this woman knew a whole lot about him.

"That'll work," he replied holding her gaze.

They stayed that way for half a beat, reading each other. Izzy smiled first.

"I'm on it," she said and left to get their beer.

"I get the impression that woman gathers intel."

"She doesn't need to gather it," Ryker stated. "It just comes to her, and she is very perceptive. Don't ever try to pull one over on her. You will not win."

He smiled sweetly at Iz as she delivered their drinks.

"Stop talking about me Ryker," she warned him. "You know how it pisses women off when you talk about them." She grinned as his face colored slightly.

"Wait, what's that about?" Maddy asked. "What'd I miss?"

"Your friend here doesn't understand that Margot Kennedy doesn't appreciate it if he jokes about her cooking ability, or lack thereof to her mother. He was in the doghouse for a couple of days. Did you grovel to her highness?"

"I made her happy," Ryker admitted.

"The diamond pendant was stunning," Izzy teased. "Expensive makeup gift."

"Damn, Ryker," Maddy gave a low whistle. "At least you can buy forgiveness with that woman. I guess that's a plus."

Jaxx took a swift drink to hide his smile. Maddy was dishing it pretty hard, but Ryker was taking it.

"I take it you don't think highly of this Margot Kennedy?" Jaxx asked.

Izzy snorted and Maddy just smiled sweetly.

"I don't need to think highly of her," Maddy said. "She thinks highly enough of herself to cover it for everyone. But I've beaten you up enough, Ryker. If she makes you happy, God love you." Maddy patted his arm as Izzy snorted again and went back to the kitchen to get their meals.

"It's a good thing I love you, Maddy. That's for sure."

14

"*R*yker, how long before that storm comes?" Maddy asked lazily, finishing her second beer, her fish dinner a happy memory.

Ryker consulted his phone.

"Not for a couple of hours, I would think. Why?"

"I am stuffed to the gills. I think I want to walk home."

"What?" asked Jaxx. "That's a long way on some busy roads. It'll be dark before you get home."

Ryker and Maddy smiled at each other.

"If you want, that's fine, but I'm happy to drive you back, Maddy."

"No, she isn't going to walk home." Jaxx looked at Ryker like he had a screw loose. "Or if you're crazy enough to do that, I'll walk with you." Walking in his work boots was not his idea of a good time, but his feet had been punished many times before in less than ideal conditions. He tried to remember what Maddy had on her feet, but he didn't want to be obvious by looking under the table.

"Jaxx, need I remind you that I don't need you to make decisions for me. I've walked home from the Mizzen Mast more times than I can count. It's not dark yet, and I'll make it home long before then."

Suddenly, Jaxx realized he was missing something. They were

messing with him. His mind worked quickly, thinking of the route they took from Maddy's to the bar, then it dawned on him.

"I could use a beach walk," said Jaxx. "Would you mind if I walked the beach to your cottage with you?"

"I don't own the beach. Anyone can walk it," Maddy said, enjoying the casual teasing they had slipped into.

"How are you going to get home from Maddy's?" Ryker asked, looking over his bottle of beer, suddenly feeling protective of his longtime friend. He liked Jaxx. He had grown to trust him, but Ryker suddenly didn't like the dynamics that would follow a walk on the beach home to Maddy's cottage leaving Jaxx without a vehicle.

"I'll drive him to your shop so he can get his truck," Maddy said firmly, picking up on Ryker's concern. "I have an early morning window delivery tomorrow," she said pointedly, "so it isn't going to be a late night." And just like that, Maddy had laid down the rules for everyone to follow.

Izzy brought the checks and slipped a card to Jaxx.

"What's this?" he asked.

"I know you're staying at the hotel out by the freeway. It's not a bad place, but it'll eat up your wages pretty quickly. Mabel Cummings has a small cottage she rents out. Her last tenant left her high and dry yesterday. Mabel counts on that rent to get her through. I think it might be a good solution for the both of you, plus the lady likes dogs." Izzy smiled at the startled look Jaxx gave her. He recovered quickly.

"Thanks, Izzy. I appreciate that. I would much rather rent a place than stay in a hotel."

"Well, I wouldn't wait. Mabel will get antsy and could have it rented by tomorrow afternoon. I'd give her a call tonight or tomorrow morning at the latest." She winked at him as she gathered the bills the three of them placed on the table. All assured her to keep the change and they said their goodnights.

"You really don't have to walk me home, Jaxx." Maddy watched as Ryker hesitated at his truck, waiting for a sign it was really okay for him to leave.

"I want to, Maddy. I've felt cooped up lately. This would be good."

"So, what you're saying is, you like long walks on the beach…"

"Right, now you need to give Ryker some kind of sign, because that man won't leave you unless he knows for certain you're totally good with this."

Maddy blew a kiss to Ryker and waved. He shook his head and grinned. Waving lazily back he crawled into his truck, a little jealous that Maddy and Jaxx still had an evening and he was going home to a lonely house. Margot would be tied up with her family until late and would need to get her beauty sleep.

"So, tell me," Jaxx said as they started down the street that lead away from the river and toward the historic downtown of Grey's Harbor, "What do you have against this Margot lady? Is she really that stuck on herself?"

"Really is, and more. She's beautiful, no, change that, she's drop dead gorgeous, is wealthy, is connected, is all the things that any woman would want to be."

"And?" asked Jaxx, knowing there had to be more.

"And she is cold. I mean, if you'd meet her, she would be kind and polite. She gives to charity. She organizes a save the puppy kind of fundraiser event every year. Outwardly she is everything a man would want in a woman. She's funny and smart."

"And?"

"And I sense there is this cold hard stone in her icy heart."

"And there it is," said Jaxx. "Has she ever done anything to give you this impression?"

"No," said Maddy, miserably. "I feel horrible thinking this, and I should probably stop giving Ryker a hard time about her. He loves her. I know he does. I'm just scared for him because I think she's going to hurt him."

Jaxx thought for a moment as they turned down the short board-walk ramp that led to the beach. When their feet hit the sand, he asked her.

"Is it because someone hurt you so badly that you're afraid the same thing will happen to your friend?"

Maddy didn't answer and didn't stop walking until she reached the ocean's edge where the relentless lapping waves had smoothed the sand into a wet, hard, surface. She looked out at the ocean, her heart squeezing in pain.

Jaxx waited, the asked question hanging in the air.

"Perhaps," she whispered, the sound carrying on the wind and waves, pulling out to sea.

"Then maybe your instinct is right, but Ryker will have to learn the same lesson you did."

"It's a very hard lesson." Maddy sighed as she turned and started walking the beach toward her cottage, Jaxx falling in step next to her. "How'd you do on your lessons?"

"Oh, I had my share of teenage heartbreak," Jaxx said lightly.

"That's not what we're talking here, is it?"

"No, it's not."

"Then what is in your soul that's eating it alive?" Maddy asked mildly, still not looking at him.

"Darlin', it would take a lifetime to tell," he said, brushing it off, meaningless.

"So, you're not ready. I respect that."

They walked on as the breeze freshened and storm clouds gathered on the horizon. The soft pastels of evening were hardening, the ocean turning a yellow gray, a warning of things to come.

Occasionally, Maddy would pick up a shell or a piece of beach glass and slip it into her pocket. As they walked the tension slowly erased from her and a calm smile settled on her face. Jaxx loved watching her relax, loved the way her lips curled upward when she was happy. He wanted to pummel the man who had hurt her so badly.

The beach curved toward the old light house, and they continued to walk as the wind picked up even more. Sea gulls and shore birds ran ahead of them snatching up bounty from the sea, and the waves moved closer as the tide continued to roll in.

As they passed the lighthouse, Jaxx sensed a change in her mood, a subtle shift. He saw her glance over to it, as the waves continued to encroach their way to the ancient building.

"What's the deal with the lighthouse?" he asked her, knowing there was a story there. He could feel it in her.

"It's the place where all the teenagers and some romantic adults trying to reclaim their youth make out. The kids build bonfires and tell ghost stories. It's as much of Grey's Harbor as the village itself."

"Ghost stories, huh? Wanna tell me one?"

The wind had increased, lifting Maddy's hair and whipping strands into her face. She reached into her pocket and pulled out an elastic band, quickly braiding her hair in a long plait down her back, securing it with her band. She did it unconsciously, just trying to tame it from the wind, but Jaxx found it incredibly sexy. He wanted to run his hands down that thick braid as he pulled her against him.

Ghost story. He needed a ghost story badly before he blew this relationship by making a move too quickly.

"Okay, listen. What do you hear?" asked Maddy.

"I hear the ocean and the gulls crying. And of course, the wind," he said, wondering just what she was getting at.

"Listen closer. Close your eyes and let your imagination run wild." Maddy waited expectantly. She could hear it. She had heard it all her life.

Jaxx listened hard. He was trained to pick out sounds that didn't belong, that signaled danger.

There, a low moaning.

He smiled. Just the sound of the wind as it whistled passed the lighthouse. The moaning increased and occasionally made a shrill shriek before settling back into a moan. It was certainly the thing teenage ghost stories were made of.

"If you mean the wind moaning like a woman, sure, I hear it. Is that our resident ghost?"

"Yes sir, that's the ghost of Madeline Abuchon. She threw herself off the lighthouse. killing herself. She was pregnant, and she's been searching for her baby all these years."

Instead of the grin Jaxx expected on Maddy's face he saw something else. She looked unhappy. Then he remembered.

"Wait, Miss Mirabelle mentioned that name. She said you are her namesake and that your cottage sits near where her home was."

"Yeah, just recently Miss Mirabelle broke it to me that when Madeline tried to kill herself, she didn't immediately die. She was pulled from the waves and she named the father of the baby with her dying breath. The baby was cut from her and somehow managed to survive. That baby's father was Cooper Grey. The baby was considered a bastard but was blessed with the Grey name and was given to a woman who had just lost her child. The Grey baby grew up to father children, who grew up to father children, and eventually I came to be. I am the eventual result of the tryst between Cooper Grey and Madeline Abuchon."

Jaxx stopped walking and put his hands on Maddy's shoulders. He could see she was pissed and confused about the whole thing.

"But what does that have to do with Miss Mirabelle?" he asked, not really wanting the explanation, knowing it somehow hurt Maddy.

"Because Miss Mirabelle is the eventual result of a legitimate marriage between Cooper Grey and someone acceptable. And now she wants to claim me as family. I am not her family," Maddy spat vehemently. "My mother worked her fingers to the bone cleaning for the likes of her family."

Jaxx had enough. He pulled Maddy to his chest and cradled the back of her head with his strong hand, the other stroking her back, protecting her.

They stood in the shadow of the lighthouse, the storm moving in around them, Madeline Abuchon crying for the loss of her baby, Maddy sobbing for the loss of her love and her identity.

15

*B*y the time they reached Maddy's cottage, the skies were threatening to open up. Spurts of rain were coming down and lightening was striking around them, the thunderclaps indicating the strikes were close.

They hit the back porch as the driving rain poured from the sky. Maddy shook off the drops laughing.

"I can't believe we made it!" Her eyes were dancing in the porch light.

"I didn't think we would." Jaxx agreed, shaking the droplets of rain from his hair.

Another loud crack made Maddy jump and squeal.

"It's not safe out here, let's get inside." He took the key from her hand and turned it in the lock. "Your hands are freezing, Maddy," he said as he ushered her inside.

"Yeah, I'm kinda cold," she admitted.

Jaxx surveyed the little cottage, spotting the fireplace.

"Is it okay if I build a fire?" he asked. "And you need to get out of those wet clothes."

"I would love it. There's some kindling and newspapers in that wooden box next to the fireplace. There's more wood on the back porch if there isn't enough in here. I'm going to put the kettle on and then be right back."

She turned to look at him as she went into her kitchen. His hair and beard still held droplets of rain, but he was crouched down in front of the fireplace intent on getting a cozy fire going. She filled the tea kettle and set it on the stove, lighting the flame underneath. When she turned back to Jaxx, he already had a small fire dancing happily as he adjusted the damper to get the right amount of draw. She smiled. Tripp never could figure out how to make that happen. Tripp was an artist, sensitive, and emotional. He was also self-centered and incredibly talented. Jaxx was a protector, capable, and strong. It was obvious he put others first. Suddenly it dawned on her that Tripp and Margot Kennedy had a lot in common. In fact, they may have been cut from the same cloth.

"What?" Jaxx asked as he glanced up at her. His face held a quizzical look as he noticed her sad smile.

"Nothing. I just had an epiphany, that's all."

"Care to share it?" he asked, fairly certain she wouldn't.

"No, I don't think so. Even better, I don't need to." She smiled and tossed over her shoulder on the way to her bedroom, "I'll be right back."

The tea kettle was whistling cheerfully as Maddy came padding back into the living room, her feet clad in thick wool socks, the rest of her in an oversized sweatshirt and yoga pants. She tossed Jaxx a heavy flannel shirt that had been her dad's.

"See if that'll fit you. It's dry, at least." Pulling two handmade ceramic mugs from the cupboard she asked, "Tea or cocoa?"

"What are you having?"

"Hot chocolate with Frangelico."

"Sounds a little girly, but what the hell."

Within minutes they were comfortably seated on the love seat that faced the fireplace. He would rather have had coffee, but it wasn't that important. Jaxx took a hesitant sip. Maddy watched him.

"Well?"

"It's delicious. Thank you. Just don't tell Tank and Ryker, or I won't ever live it down."

"Tank and Ryker love cocoa with Frangelico."

"They drink this?"

"We all did. Maeve, Ryker, Tank, Bridger. When we were kids, we would take it to our bonfires. Our parents thought it was sweet that we were drinking hot chocolate, the picture of good kids. What they didn't realize was we would lace it with whatever we could get our hands on. Bridger's mom always had Frangelico in the house, so we would use it a lot."

"I don't think I've met Bridger."

"Bridger Cadigan. His family owns the marina up the river. A lot of fishing charters run out of there, and Bridger builds wooden boats and sells them."

"Wooden boats like kayaks and canoes?"

"No, well, yes and no. He does those, but he builds sailboats and motorboats, too."

"That's like a lost art."

"He's an artist in his own right. You should see them sometime."

"I'd like to. I bet it was a sight to see, you guys all around a fire on the beach, the lighthouse in the shadows, drinking a hot girly drink and scaring each other."

Maddy smiled with the fond memories.

"The thing is, we were young and had no business drinking. When we got older, we were typical teenagers sneaking beer and wine and roasting clams in the fire."

"It sounds like you had a wonderful childhood, Maddy. Did you grow up in this house?"

"No, we lived in a small house in town. My parents weren't wealthy. Mom cleaned the houses of the haves and dad worked in heating and air conditioning. We just had this house for the summers."

"Your parents rented this place for the whole summer? How'd they afford that?" Jaxx voiced the question that Maddy had wondered about for years.

"Honestly, I don't know. I don't even know when this cottage became theirs. I just know that when dad died and I had to go through his things, the deed to this cottage was there."

"Your mom passed first?"

"Yeah, she died of breast cancer. They didn't catch it. She went fast." Maddy was silent for a minute, thinking of that time, the news and losing her mom within months.

"I'm sorry, Maddy."

"Thank you."

"And your dad?"

"Dad died of carbon monoxide poisoning."

"What?"

"When I was in college. Apparently, there was something wrong with the furnace. He died in his sleep. That's why I sold that house. I couldn't bear the thought of staying there."

"Maddy, didn't you just tell me your dad was in the business."

"Yes. I did. Don't go there." She looked at him steadily.

He sipped his cocoa and watched her over the rim of his cup. There was so much pain in this girl. The layers were peeling away slowly.

Her eyes rose to meet his. A challenge.

"And you? Your history?"

"Not much to tell. Parents are still alive. Mom wishes I would come home to Colorado. Dad leaves me alone. We talk once a week. It's enough. After my military stint, I moved back to Colorado."

"And what drove you away again?" Maddy asked, moving her hand to his sleeve. She sensed his change. She understood how Betty knew the shift in her master. They could both feel it.

Jaxx took a deep breath. He didn't talk about it. Didn't want to.

"You don't have to, Jaxx, but it's only fair. You aren't the only one who can sense pain and who might want to protect and fix it."

"It's my job," he said stubbornly.

"It may be, but there is sometimes more than one person with the same job."

"True, but it's not your job to protect me."

"I don't get a say in this?"

"No, you don't.

"Then can I at least try to understand you if not protect you?"

She waited. The storm raged outside, sand and rain pelting the side of the cottage. Her mind flipped for a second to the ancient foundations, the remains of Madeline Abuchon's cottage just a few yards from her own, and the strange fact that she lived here and Mirabelle's hints that there was a lot more to her story.

Her mind moved back to Jaxx. He was staring into the fire.

"I was married once. I had a wife and a daughter. They died. End of story."

"Jaxx. I…there are no words. I'm sorry, but…"

"Maddy, I know. It's okay."

"My guess is you're done. You don't want to talk."

"I don't. Really, Maddy, I don't."

"Okay, I can respect that. Can you throw another log on the fire?"

Jaxx poked the fire and added a log and they settled back in the couch in silence.

"Maddy, Miss Mirabelle acts like she has an ace in the hole, like she has some power over you that you don't know about. Do you have any idea what it is?"

"No, I don't. I couldn't care less what Mirabelle has to say."

"I understand that, but if you knew, if you understood before she decided to spring it on you, then you would take the power away from her. She wouldn't have any hold on you."

"She doesn't have a hold on me now," Maddy protested.

"I think she does. I think she very carefully planted a seed in you, and that seed is starting to grow. It's going to start weaving its tendrils into your waking moments, making you wonder what piece of the puzzle you're missing."

Maddy thought back to the few minutes ago when her mind left Jaxx and she pondered the old foundation. He was right. It was invading her thoughts. The thing is, she dreaded knowing the truth. She was afraid it was going to change everything once she discovered the things that Mirabelle was hinting at.

She shivered uncontrollably at the thought. Jaxx took her cocoa mug from her, setting it on the low table in front of the couch. Then he gently turned her, pulling her back against him so she lay against his chest, his arms wrapped around her, his hand stroking her hair. And for the second time that day, he sheltered her as she wept.

16

"*M*addy," Jaxx whispered, his lips brushing her forehead.

"Hmmm?"

"Wake up, honey. You're going to have to get me to my truck if you don't want Ryker jumping to conclusions." The last thing he wanted was to tarnish Maddy's reputation, especially when there was nothing gained in return.

"I don't care," she murmured, her breath warm against her father's flannel shirt.

"You might feel differently in the light of day, darlin'."

"I feel just fine the way we are," she said sleepily.

He groaned. She had no idea what she was doing to him right then. While she had slept, he had turned over things in his mind, working through all the possibilities. He knew Mirabelle must have a bombshell to drop on Maddy, and he was going to do everything in his power not to let that happen. Working through all that had help keep his mind off the beautiful, vulnerable woman who was sleeping on his chest, but now his body and mind were at full attention.

She purred like a cat and stretched, reaching her face up to nuzzle his beard. She was teasing him. She was soft and sleepy and incredibly seductive as she looked up at him through her long dark lashes.

He shifted slightly and lifted her chin bringing her lips to his. She responded with a soft, sleepy kiss. He pulled her on top of him and she stretched out his length, her wool socks soft against his bare feet. He had shed his boots an hour ago, slowly and carefully without waking her.

He kissed her and explored her mouth until both of their nerves were tingling with excitement. When he was certain she was completely awake, he pulled away and looked up at her. Her braid, messy from the rain and the attention from his hands, fell forward like a silky rope. She looked down at him expectantly.

"I need you to drive me to my truck," he said.

"I might need something else," she replied, snuggling down, her cheek against his chest.

This was totally unlike her. She didn't even know this man, not really. She knew he made her feel safe, and she knew Ryker trusted him. She knew that he had loved and lost, and she was fairly certain he had taken a life. She also knew he had given life. She was tired of hurting, and she just wanted to throw caution to the wind.

Jaxx ran his hands along her back, soothing her. He knew what she wanted. She had made it clear. He groaned a little. He wanted it, too. He wanted to explore every curve of her body, to know her, to protect her, but he was also a cautious, smart man. He knew it wasn't right.

"Maddy, honey, you can take me home tonight, or you can take me home in the morning. Either way, we're not going to take this any further than we have."

He felt her stiffen, and it hurt him. He hurried to reassure her.

"It's not that I don't want to. I want to in the worst way, but it isn't right. Neither of us is ready, and I don't want us to regret what we've done. I don't want to hurt you like you've been hurt before. Do you understand, Maddy?"

She nodded against his chest, not wanting to look at him.

"Maddy, look at me."

She waited a minute then raised herself so she could see his face, look in his eyes.

"Maddy do you understand?" He watched her earnestly, a soft smile on his lips.

"I understand, and you're right. I don't know what came over me," she said, a little embarrassed.

"No, no, don't be embarrassed. There's nothing to be embarrassed about. You're beautiful and desirable, and I would love to lay you back and treat you the way you deserve, but not tonight. Not when you're feeling the way you do, vulnerable and lost." He pulled her down to him and kissed her again, reassuring her that he wanted her, but he was strong enough for the both of them to resist her.

A minute later, Maddy pulled herself away from Jaxx. She reluctantly stood and stretched the kinks out of her back. Jaxx felt the tug of disappointment despite his brain telling him he did the right thing.

She disappeared into the bathroom, then he heard a door open in the hall. She came back with a handful of bedding.

"Hop up, cowboy, and help me open this couch. It makes into a bed." He did what he was told and then took the bedding from her. "You can stay here for the night. I really don't relish going out in the storm then driving back all by myself. It wouldn't be safe," she teased.

"What about Ryker?"

"Ryker won't be a problem," she said with a smile. "It's Tank you're going to have to worry about."

She bent down and gave him a kiss.

"Goodnight. I hope you sleep well. There's an unopened toothbrush in the top right drawer in the bathroom. You'll find towels on the shelf. Please help yourself to anything you need, and I'll see you in the morning."

"Thanks, Maddy. Sleep well." He heard her pad down the hall and climb into her own bed. He was tired and he looked forward to hitting the pillow. He found the promised toothbrush, and in minutes he was stretched out on the pull out bed, staring at the dying embers in the fireplace. He had just drifted off to sleep when he heard Maddy's frenzied voice.

"Jaxx. Wake up. How could we have forgotten her?"

"Who?" Jaxx asked, sitting up and trying to access the situation. *Was there danger?*

"Betty? You left Betty alone."

Jaxx got his adrenaline under control then smiled that she remembered his dog and was worried.

"I called Johnny-Ray at the hotel. He's already tried to claim my dog as his own. He takes her out and takes care of her whenever I need him to. I called him while you were sleeping. Betty has been walked, fed, and tucked into bed. All is well. Now go get your beauty sleep."

She smiled at him and waved goodnight, satisfied that all was indeed well.

17

*M*addy pulled into the parking lot at Ryker's construction office not at all surprised to see Ryker and Tank already there. She plastered a huge smile on her face and waved at them.

"You're gonna have some explainin' to do," she teased Jaxx.

Jaxx groaned as he caught the murderous look on Tank's face.

"I don't suppose you have my back?" he asked, with an attempt at his most pathetic face.

"Sorry, buddy. No matter how hard you try, you could never look pathetic. And now, I'm going to make it even harder on you." She leaned over and gave him a kiss. At first, he looked surprised, and then he grinned. She had bested him, but just for a moment. He looked out the front window of her car and gave Ryker and Tank a one-minute sign, holding his index finger up. He noticed Tank was fuming. Then he proceeded to kiss Maddy thoroughly, taking his time until she squirmed. *That's better*, he thought.

"See you later?" he asked.

"I would expect you by my house fairly soon with a window. Right?"

"Absolutely." He slowly unwound himself from Maddy's small car.

The woman needed a truck, he thought, then he sauntered his way over to Ryker and Tank, waving goodbye carelessly over his shoulder.

Maddy pulled the car out of the parking lot and left with a wave at the men and a cheery toot of her horn leaving Jaxx to fend for himself.

Maddy unlocked her studio and went to work cleaning and photographing her latest order of bowls. She catalogued the entire order noting the size, design, glass, and firing schedules for each of the pieces. She was debating whether to ship the order or make a trip to Nag's Head to make the delivery in person. She was leaning that way, but she hated to miss time in her studio, especially with all the windows to complete. Still, shipping had its risks.

Two hours later, Ryker, Tank, and Jaxx showed up at her studio door with the next window. They helped her unpack it and lay it flat.

"How does bacon and eggs sound? Do you guys have time?" she asked. Curiosity was killing her. She wanted to know how Jaxx had fared with her friends.

"Works for me," Ryker said. The others nodded in agreement.

Maddy led them into the cottage and Ryker immediately began to make coffee. Tank opened the pantry and pulled out a loaf of bread to make toast.

"I take it this is normal ritual for you guys," Jaxx said, feeling a little left out.

"It was until Tripp. That put a stop to it. This is the first time since he left," Tank said, plugging in the toaster.

Maddy stilled, her head in the fridge, the bacon half retrieved.

"Shit," said Tank. "Sorry, Maddy. It just came out."

Jaxx moved over to Maddy's side.

"I'm guessing you need these eggs?" he asked as he pulled a large basket of brown eggs out of the refrigerator.

"Yes, thank you," she said, not looking at him. She straightened up holding a butcher wrapped hunk of bacon.

Tank handed Jaxx a huge cast iron skillet and the four of them got to work making breakfast.

"hy did you let Tripp stop you from having breakfasts with your friends?"

Jaxx had his hands buried in soapy dishwater as Maddy dried the dishes he handed her. Ryker and Tank were heading over to inspect the roof repair at Cadigan's Marina and Maddy was going drop Jaxx at his truck when they were done cleaning up.

"I honestly don't know," she admitted. "He just came into my life and we isolated ourselves, concentrating on each other and our art."

"What happened?" Jaxx asked casually as he finished the last plate.

"Success. His."

He dried his hands and took the towel from her, hanging it on the hook.

"But you're a success, Maddy. What do you mean, his success?"

"He said he needed to be in New York, that his art needed a large urban area, a gallery. Grey's Harbor wasn't the place for him to grow. A gallery contacted him, and he left."

"Maddy, I'm sorry."

"To be fair, he asked me to go with him, but I couldn't. I couldn't leave here, my place by the sea, my home."

"Maddy, how did he ask you to go with him?" Jaxx lifted her chin so she had to look in his eyes. She lowered her lashes. Avoiding. "That's what I thought. No strings attached, right? Just leave your home with no commitments from him."

She nodded miserably, extracting herself from him. She moved to look out the back window and onto the ocean, the waves pulling the pain away.

"You made the right choice. You know that don't you?"

She was still.

"Then why does it still hurt so much?" she whispered.

"Because Maddy, you don't love casually. You love with your whole heart. When you do that, you hurt more, but Maddy, when it's right, it will be so right with you. You deserve to have someone love you back the same way."

She sighed then straightened her shoulders and put on a sunny smile.

He recognized she was done. Enough was enough.

"Are you ready to take me to my truck?"

"Sure. So how are you going to spend the rest of your Saturday?'

"I thought about taking Betty to the beach. Is that allowed?"

"It is. Just don't let her be a nuisance."

"You want to come, or do you need to work on that window?"

"I would love to come. The window can wait until later, and you can tell me how you sweet talked Tank into not killing you."

Maddy drove Jaxx to his truck then followed him to his hotel to pick up Betty. She was ecstatic to see Maddy, wiggling her butt, her tail wagging and trying to be polite the whole time. Maddy scratched Betty's ears while Jaxx took a minute to call the number Izzy gave him to inquire about the cottage for rent. Mabel told him that it was still available and invited him to stop by with his dog for a "look see."

"Do you want to come with me to see the cottage?" Jaxx asked, as they walked to the truck, Betty dancing happily between them.

"We can just go to my house, drop the vehicles and walk the beach to get there if you want."

"Wait, this cottage is on the beach?"

"I'm pretty sure it is second from the beach, but it's backyard is sort of open to it. It would be perfect for Betty."

They parked at Maddy's cottage then walked on the dune path to the ocean, Betty trotting happily between them. She frolicked happily in the waves, biting the sea foam and nosing crab holes coming up with sand stuck to her face. She looked at Jaxx and Maddy, ran in circles and chased the waves again. She was delighted with the way the day was turning out.

Jaxx pulled Maddy's hand into his as they walked and enjoyed Betty's antics, the sea soothing both of their souls.

A short time after they passed the lighthouse they turned away from the ocean and walked a wooden sidewalk to a small stand of cottages.

Most of them were old but well kept, painted soft coastal colors with wide porches. Jaxx checked the addresses stopping in front of compact shake shingle cottage. Maddy was right, it was the second one from the end of the street. As he stepped up on the porch ready to knock on the door, it opened, and a stooped elderly woman peered up at him.

"Ms. Cummings?" Jaxx asked.

"Mabel." She offered her hand. "You must be Jaxx," she said, her faded blue eyes twinkling, "and this must be Betty."

Betty sat primly in front of Mabel and offered her paw.

"I like her. She's well-mannered," Mabel declared. She looked keenly at Jaxx. "Are you well-mannered, young man?"

"Very much, ma'am," he answered solemnly.

Mabel looked him over again waiting for him to squirm under her examination. She had been a high school librarian in her day, and she still could deliver the look. Jaxx stood up calmly to it, his lips turned up in a slight smile.

Mabel was charmed. She turned her attention to Maddy.

"Maddy Grey, I haven't seen you in years. I heard that artist fellow you were dating went to New York. Good riddance, I say. He was stuck up."

Maddy looked startled, not used to someone being so blunt about her breakup with Tripp.

"Don't look surprised. Surely you know when you're my age you just speak your mind. Are you and this Jaxx fellow an item?" The ocean colored eyes peered into hers, seeking an answer.

Betty watched with interest.

"We're just friends, Mabel."

"Humph. It's obvious he likes you dear. You should take advantage of it. Well come on in, Jaxx, and see if this place agrees with you."

She turned abruptly and led them into the cottage, not looking around to see if they followed.

"After you," Jaxx gestured to Maddy and Betty. They followed Mabel inside.

The cottage was charming, but not overwhelmingly so.

"This will do just fine," he stated, before he even moved from the living room.

"Jaxx, you haven't seen the cottage yet, just the living room," Maddy protested as she moved toward the kitchen.

"The man knows what he needs and what he doesn't," Mabel said. "That's a good thing."

Jaxx and Mabel struck an agreement and Mabel produced the lease. While they took care of business, Maddy wandered around the cottage checking it over to see what Jaxx was getting himself into. It was small but neat and clean, perfect for his needs. There was a nice screened back porch. Betty decided it was the perfect place to flop down on the tile floor and watch the activity on the beach. Maddy settled into an upholstered glider and waited with Betty as Jaxx and Mabel finished their business.

"I understand you're repairing Mirabelle Grey's damaged stained-glass windows." Mabel said as she stepped onto the back porch, Jaxx following close behind. She eased herself into a porch rocker and waited for Maddy to answer her.

"Yes, I am. Has that become the talk of the town for some reason?"

"No, I've just wondered how long it would be before old Mirabelle got you back into that house."

"What do you mean?"

"Why, you used to play there as a child, when your mother cleaned for Mirabelle. Your mother stopped working for her and Mirabelle was very unhappy about it. I knew someday she would get you back there."

"I don't remember that at all," Maddy said, stubbornly.

Jaxx sat down on the glider next to her and took her hand, sensing she was becoming a little distressed.

"Of course, you don't remember, you were not much older than a toddler. You were probably too young to retain any of those memories."

"I don't understand, why would I go with my mom while she cleaned?"

"Mirabelle insisted. She always wanted you near her."

"But why?"

"Ms. Cummings, what is it that Miss Mirabelle is holding over Maddy's head? Mirabelle keeps hinting at some big secret. I don't want Maddy blindsided by this, so if you know something, I would appreciate it if you would share it."

Jaxx gave the old woman a steady look. Mabel considered it for a minute, rolling the idea around in her mind. Then she looked over at the dark-haired beauty. The resemblance to the portrait that hung in the little Grey's Harbor historical society of Madeline Abuchon was startling. She sat quietly, collecting herself.

"Do you know your family tree?"

Maddy nodded her head. "I didn't know that I was descended from Cooper Grey and Madeline Abuchon until just recently. Miss Mirabelle shared that with me. She seems to think that I am a Grey like she's a Grey. I'm not. I'm just Maddy who happens to have the last name of Grey. It doesn't mean anything."

"Yes, Maddy. You are a Grey. Zachariah Grey gave the baby of Madeline Abuchon the Grey name so that his descendants would be also called Grey. You are a Grey in your own right, but you don't share the entitlement that a few of the family seem to have. Maddy, there are a whole lot of good people in the Grey clan, even ones who are wealthy. Don't judge someone just because they have money."

"I don't. I just don't care about them one way or another. It's just a name."

"I understand that, but to someone like Miss Mirabelle, it's more than that. It's a legacy. Maddy, Miss Mirabelle was married to a man she loved with all her heart. She was beautiful, sparkling, and full of life, and she was the belle of the town. Her wedding was the event of the social season, a marriage made in heaven, a uniting of soulmates. Wherever Mirabelle and Drummond went the world seemed to shine brighter. People loved being around them because they were so happy and so in love. When Mirabelle became pregnant with her first child, she was ecstatic. No expense was spared for the nursery. Nannies were interviewed and rejected, and Mirabelle grew more beautiful with each passing day.

"Sadly, she miscarried that child. She fell into a deep depression that lasted a year, until she discovered she was pregnant again. She took to her bed, determined that this child would not have the same fate, but sadly, she lost that one, too. And the next, and the next. Eventually, she didn't even become pregnant again. Her marriage fell apart and she shut herself in that big, old house."

"That's horrible," Maddy said, her eyes bright with tears. Jaxx squeezed her hand, afraid that the rest of this story was going to go down an even darker place. He could feel it in his bones, and his body started to kick into protection mode.

Mabel sensed the shift in Jaxx and nodded, affirming that the worst was yet to come.

"I feel so badly for her. It's just so horrible," Maddy repeated, at a loss for words, "but what does any of that have to do with me?"

"The day you were born, Mirabelle visited your parents in the hospital. You were the descendant of Madeline Abuchon, but also of Cooper Grey, just like she was. She attached herself to you and your parents. She was determined to be part of your life. She always felt that she had been punished for the sins of the fathers, for Cooper Grey abandoning Madeline. I think she thought that if she atoned for their sins, she would somehow be forgiven, and she would also have a baby in her life."

"Wait, how would I be in her life? My parents wouldn't have anything to do with her. This doesn't make sense."

"Maddy, you don't have to hear the rest of this if you don't want to," Jaxx said, turning her to look at him. "What happened in the past doesn't matter. Mirabelle doesn't have any hold on you or your life."

"No, I want to hear the rest. I want to know what secrets Mirabelle keeps hinting at. I want this done once and for all," she said, the determination in her voice not matching the pale fear on her face.

Betty whined from where she was laying and got up to push her huge head in Maddy's lap. Maddy's hand moved to scratch the big dog's ears as Betty leaned heavily against her.

"Mirabelle offered your parents a very large sum of money for naming rights," Mabel said simply.

"Naming rights?" Maddy echoed.

"Correct. Your parents collected the cash and Mirabelle was able to name you. She named you Madeline Anne Grey, after Madeline Abuchon and herself."

"I'm named after Mirabelle?"

"Yes, dear, Mirabelle Anne Grey."

"And my parents allowed that to happen? How do you know all this?" Maddy demanded, getting angry now.

"I know this because I was Mirabelle's best friend. I was by her side for the loss of every one of those babies. I sat with her in her depressions, until one day she even shut the door on me. When her husband left, she shut me out of her life and closed the doors to that beautiful house which has seen so much life, so many parties. Mirabelle was alive but dead inside. It wasn't until your mother was pregnant with you that Mirabelle came out of her fog. She contacted me again. Told me her plans. She was so excited that you were going to be born. She was convinced that you were the baby that would bring an end to the pain and heartache she had lived with."

"That's crazy," Jaxx said, moving his arm to Maddy's shoulders, pulling her closer to him.

"Yes, I think Mirabelle went a little mad. I don't know, maybe she thought she could buy you from your parents, but they wouldn't have it, of course, so instead she came up with the offer of naming rights. I believe your parents finally took the money so that you could have a better life. They were simple people, but with Mirabelle's money, they could provide better things for you. They could be sure you could go to college one day if you wished.

"As you grew, you used to spend time at the house. Mirabelle would let your parents stay at the summer cottage and they would let Mirabelle have time with you. Your mother would clean her house so she could keep an eye on you, and Mirabelle would play dress up with you or have tea parties."

Just for a second, Maddy had a memory flash of sitting at a small white table covered with a tiny delicate tea set. Vivid sun-filled colors lay in a dapple pattern across the table.

Stained glass.

"One day, your mother overheard Mirabelle telling you that she was your grandmother. That was the last straw. Your mother took you away, never to bring you back. Mirabelle was heartbroken. She begged, threatened, and screamed at your parents to bring you back to her. She signed over the deed to the cottage at Grey's Landing to your father to be held for you, but your parents still didn't budge. You were done seeing that woman."

Maddy sat stunned.

Betty whined and shoved her nose under Maddy's hand. Maddy scratched her ears absently.

Jaxx was the first to speak. "Is there anything more that this poor girl doesn't know? If so, now is the time to spill it." His jaw was tense, and his mind was working, trying to figure out how to protect Maddy from this world of hurt that had been heaped on her.

"Not much that I know of. They finally came to an agreement that Maddy would still spend her summers at the Grey's Landing cottage so that Mirabelle could watch her grow up, but she wasn't to have contact with her anymore. Your parents threatened to take out a restraining order and that stopped Mirabelle in her tracks."

"What do you mean Mirabelle could still watch me grow up?"

"She would spend hours sitting in that tower at the top of the house watching the beach, trying to get a glimpse of you. You were on that beach quite a lot, and she kept an eye on you. She made it her business to know everything about you, what you did, and who your friends were."

Maddy's face grew even colder. She shuddered at the idea that she had been spied on her entire life from the tower she had caught glimpses of as a child. Even more disturbing, her parents allowed it to happen.

Mabel saw the anger start to bubble below the surface.

"Maddy, don't be too hard on Mirabelle or your parents. Everyone did what they did because they loved you."

"Parents who love their children don't sell them for money."

"Parents who are kind loving people, who care about someone

who is hurting might be able to see another side, my dear. Everyone knew about Mirabelle and the loss of all her babies. This is a tight knit village; we share in each other's joys and sorrow."

"I didn't know," Maddy said stubbornly

"Of course not. Time marches on. Generations die and are born, and the stories fade." Mabel tsked, "Your generation doesn't know much of the history of Grey's Harbor. I would guess you've never even set foot in the historical society building." Mabel raised her eyebrows with the question.

"No, I haven't," Maddy admitted.

"Well, I suggest you do it someday. It's open every Saturday until five o'clock. I'm sorry but Betty isn't allowed." She said pointedly, making the not so subtle inference that today would be a good day for that activity. "Now, I'm going to leave you. Jaxx, you have the key and the cottage is ready for you. The historical society is one block down, two blocks to the left. Admission is free."

As she rose from her chair, Jaxx jumped up to assist her. Mabel waved him away. She walked to Betty and pat the dog on the head. Betty's tail thumped on the porch floor, happy for all the attention. Mabel turned her kind, wise eyes on Maddy.

"I know you are hurt, dear. I know this is a lot to take in. I told Mirabelle to come clean to you before she asked you to fix her windows, but she does things in her own way and in her own time. Please don't be too hard on her. She's had a life full of tragedy and pain. You understand a little about pain, having a man walk out on you, but the pain of losing child after child is something no woman should have to bear. She tried to find happiness and atone for the sins of her ancestors, but she botched that up badly. She loved you too much. That's her only sin, Maddy. Please think before you judge anyone too harshly."

Maddy's eyes were still hard and cold, but she heard what Mabel said. Mabel smiled and patted her hand.

"You have a good heart. I know you'll do the right thing." Mabel gave a little wave and crossed into the cottage and left out the front door.

Jaxx crossed to where a stunned Maddy sat. He crouched in front of her taking her hands in his. They were as cold as ice.

"Come on, Maddy. Let's go out to the beach and warm up. The sun will feel good, and I think you need those ocean waves.

She nodded miserably. Jaxx stood and pulled her to her feet. She looked so small and destroyed somehow. His heart hurt for her and he wrapped his arms around her and pulled her against his chest. As strong and he was, as trained as he was, he could not protect her from the hurt she was feeling. There was no one to train his sniper sights on. No real enemy to eliminate, just a haunting past that ripped at this beautiful girl's heart. Part of him wanted to destroy Mirabelle for the hurt she had caused, but Maddy's parents were culpable, too. If they had just been honest and not have hidden the truth. If there hadn't been secrets, then Maddy wouldn't be dealing with any of this pain now. She just would have had a rich close relative. He thought about it harder. *Something didn't add up.*

When she pulled away from him, her eyes were dry. He wasn't sure if she had been crying, and he was waiting her out, but the eyes that looked up at him were full of steel. She was ready for a fight. He just wondered who the real enemy was.

"Let's walk," she said.

"Okay, where?" he answered willing to go anywhere with her. Betty fell in next to them, determined not to be left behind.

"First, we hit the beach. I need to clear my head. Then we hit the Cathead Diner for one of Maeve's malts. I need to fill my soul. Then to the historical society because I need to feed my curiosity. Are you up for it?"

"Absolutely. Betty isn't allowed at the historical society, though."

"I know, but she is allowed on the sidewalk patio at the Cathead, so we can do that first. Is it okay to drop her back here then?"

"Sure, she'll just snooze until we get back."

They walked back to the beach. Jaxx started to reach for Maddy's hand but read her body language. She was turned in to herself and that's where she wanted to be at the moment. He had been there. Had stayed there for years. He understood her hurt. And Mirabelle's.

Losing a child can unhinge a person. Losing more than one was unimaginable.

They walked in silence, Betty matching their mood. Occasionally she rushed a group of seagulls and then came running back to them, her mouth pulled into a wide grin.

"Betty is glad to be out of a hotel room," Maddy said, coming out of her silence.

"She sure is. She's going to love that back porch."

Suddenly, Betty stilled and moved in front of Jaxx and Maddy. A low growl rumbled in her chest.

Two boys were running straight toward them. They were both looking over their shoulders as they ran watching the kites they were trying to get up in the air. They had no idea they were on a collision course with a huge dog and two people.

"Easy, Betty," Jaxx commanded,

"Garret, Gavin, head's up," Maddy called out laughing as the boys pulled up short of crashing into them.

"Oh my gosh, Maddy. Sorry about that." Garret's face colored as he stammered out his apology. Gavin's eyes were taking in the dog.

"It's okay guys. I just don't think Betty would have taken to being tackled by you two."

"Betty? The dog's name is Betty?" Gavin said in the unabashed way only a kid could do.

"Yeah, Betty," said Jaxx. "It's just how it is."

"Can I pet her?" Garret asked, his kite forgotten in the sand.

"Sure," said Jaxx, "Betty, sit."

Betty obediently plopped her butt down in the sand and subjected herself to the happy hands of the twin boys.

"Hey, Maddy, Mom loved that garden sign. Thanks for the suggestion. She said she loves being able to look at the stained glass in the garden with her flowers around it. It was a great birthday present suggestion."

"Anytime boys. I am happy to help," she smiled indulgently at Garret and Gavin, suddenly remembering that their mother was a Grey, too.

"Good, cause we're gonna need a great idea come Christmas, too. Thanks for letting us pet your dog, mister," Garret said, as he and his brother picked up their kites and started running down the beach again, this time checking their path a little more carefully.

"Cute kids," Jaxx said. "Polite for young teenagers."

"Yeah, they're good kids. Mabel is a smart lady. She reminded me that there are a lot of people who are Grey's who are good people. Ready for that malt?"

She turned to face him; her lips quirked up in a smile. He loved that she bounced back quickly. It was like she had to process the information then figure out how to proceed, but she wasn't going to let it alter her.

Maeve greeted her warmly when they arrived at the Cathead. After some quick introductions, Maeve disappeared into the diner to make their malts and Jaxx and Maddy settled into a bistro table, Betty at their feet.

"So, what's next?" Jaxx asked her. He was willing to do whatever she wanted, but he didn't want to see her destroy herself by going on a quest for knowledge. He wished he could do some reconnaissance work first, maybe soften the blow, but she looked determined.

"I'm going to the historical society. There is something there that Mabel wants me to see. It's almost as if I am supposed to figure this all out myself."

"Maybe, and I'll help you, but you don't have to do it all at once, if you need time to digest what you learn."

"No, Jaxx, I do. I want this over and done with. I want to lay this to rest along with a whole lot of other baggage in my life and move forward." She looked at him intently. She had come to the conclusion that she wanted to move past Tripp, too, and consider a new chapter. Jaxx figured into that. At least she hoped.

Jaxx smiled at her and took her hand. He could read people and he liked what he was seeing. When Maeve came out with their malts, she paused to look at them. It was obvious she was looking at two people who were very much interested in each other, and she couldn't be happier for her friend. Tripp had done a number on Maddy, and

Maeve had been worried. Maddy still looked keyed up, but Maeve could tell that Jaxx had a good effect on her.

"Here you go, guys. Can I get you anything else?"

"Aww Maeve, you made it extra chocolatey. Thanks, I love you for it."

Maeve squeezed her shoulder and Maddy suddenly remembered Tank.

"Oh, Jaxx, whatever happened with Tank this morning?" Maddy asked sweetly. Maeve laughed. She had already gotten an earful from Tank about what he thought of the situation last night.

"Nothing. He told me he would kill me if I hurt you, and I said that was fine. We shook hands and moved on. We're men, not teenage girls. We understand each other. It's good. Oh, and Maeve, if he ever hurts you, just let me know. I have experience on my side," Jaxx said mildly, but the meaning was perfectly clear. Maddy had never felt safer.

"Maeve," Maddy said, stopping Maeve from leaving the table.

"Yeah, honey?"

"Have you ever been to the historical society?"

"Sure, but it's been years, why?"

"Just curious." Maddy said, the wheels turning in her head.

Jaxx watched her. She looked like a woman who was planning a defense.

"That is not the question of someone who is just curious," Maeve said with air quotes.

"I just wondered what all is there? Is there anything interesting to look at?"

"Sure, they have a wonderful display of clothing through the years, most of it donated by some or other member of the Grey family. Other families of the upper crust are represented, too. There are old property maps, photographs, and portraits of the more prominent citizens."

Maeve looked at her friend with concern. It was obvious something was bothering her. Her eyes met Jaxx, and he looked grave. Something bad was happening.

"Maddy, honey, you know I'm here if you need me. Any time day or night, you can call. You've always known that, right?"

"I do," Maddy said with a wane smile. "And you've never let me down. It's just this road I need to travel by myself."

Maeve glanced at Jaxx again. Was he included? Jaxx shrugged. He wasn't sure either. Maeve leaned down and caught Maddy in a hug. "I'm going to call you tonight, just to check on you. Okay?"

Maddy nodded. "Thanks, Maeve. I'm sorry. I'm not trying to shut you out. I'm just out of sorts and have a lot of things to process. I'll explain later." She leaned over and took a long draw from the straw. "I'll tell you this malt is definitely helping. You're the very best."

Maeve gave her a final hug and made her way back into the diner to attend to her inside customers as Maddy leaned back in her chair with her eyes closed sipping her malt.

Jaxx let her be. He could wait for her as long as she needed.

When they finished their malts, Jaxx excused himself to go inside to the restroom, leaving Maddy to stay with Betty. As he left the men's room, Maeve walked up to him.

"I don't know what's going on with Maddy, but if you have anything to do with her mood, we're going to have a problem. I know you and Tank have an agreement, but I'm her best friend and she has never shut me out. Now, I have a problem with this. She was hurting before you came along, but she was getting better. Now she is spiraling down, and I don't like it."

Jaxx waited until Maeve was done then he steadied his eyes at her. He knew he was capable of calming her down in seconds, but he didn't want to. She was right to be worried about her friend. What he wanted to convey was she could trust him. She returned his gaze, reading his face.

"Maeve, I came into this town looking for a job and a place to be left alone, just me and my dog. I had no intention of seeking out the friendship of a woman. But here I am, and Maddy has become my business. You're right. She's hurting. It's up to her to tell the story, but I promise you, I'm going to be there to catch her when she falls. I don't let my friends down. I carry them and never leave them in battle. Do you understand? I will carry Maddy. I promise you that."

Maeve considered what his said, sizing him up. Tank was right. This guy was straight up and dangerous. It was good to have him on Maddy's side.

He asked for the bill and settled up, then asked for Maeve's phone number and gave her his. Just in case, he told her. She felt even better about him after that.

"Now what do you want to do?" Jaxx asked Maddy as he returned to her and she stood up from her chair.

"I'm ready to go to the historical society. I need to go there. I think there is something for me to see there."

"Do you want me to go with you, or do you want to be alone?" Jaxx asked.

"Honestly, I don't know," Maddy said, looking confused.

"Okay, let's head back to the cottage and drop Betty off. Then you can decide from there."

Together they walked to the cottage, Maddy deep in thought. Betty trotted next to her, glancing at her face and Jaxx's, back and forth. She knew something was wrong, she could read the tension, but she wasn't sure how to fix it.

Jaxx unlocked the cottage and Betty bounded in already at home in her new place. She trotted into the bathroom and helped herself to a cold drink from the toilet.

"And I was wondering how to leave her some water when we went to the historical society. Problem solved."

"So, you want me to come?" Jaxx asked quietly.

"I do."

Making sure Betty was settled they made the short walk to the Grey's Harbor Historical Society as the gilt sign in front of the historic Queen Anne style home announced proudly. Maddy took a deep breath, straightened her shoulders, and made her way up the steps to the large, ornate front porch. Over the front door was a beautiful stained-glass transom. Maddy smiled at it, admiring the quality workmanship. The window was exquisite.

The front door was ornate with an embossed doorknob and extensive carving. Maddy's hand trembled as she reached out and turned the knob. As the door opened, a bell tinkled merrily, welcoming them and alerting the staff that a visitor had entered.

The house gleamed with polished wood, crystal, and beautiful antique furniture. There was a card rack and a register book on a small desk in the entryway. Maddy ignored the register but picked up the self-guide instruction card which prompted her to begin her tour by turning left.

They wandered through the rooms, Maddy tense, not knowing what she was looking for. The house worked its charm on her, though, and before too long, she was enjoying the atmosphere, the examples of stained glass, and the maps and letters displayed on the walls. Jaxx stood off to her side, following her lead, letting her explore as she wanted.

As they turned into a small room toward the back of the first floor, Maddy's eyes fell on a prominent portrait and she stopped cold in her tracks. Unlike the portrait at Miss Mirabelle's that had a slight resemblance to her, she was staring back at herself painted during another era. The same thick, dark long tresses, spilling down over creamy shoulders. Her dress had slid off her shoulders and the curve of her breasts was prominent, her right nipple threatening to peek out from the edge of the gauzy white fabric. Her dark eyes were flashing, full of life, and exuding sexuality. Maddy crossed the room and stood below the portrait. Madeline Abuchon.

Jaxx looked at the portrait and back at Maddy. It was as if it were the same person down to the birth mark on her right cheek. The only difference was that Madeline Abuchon's eyes held no sadness, only a zest for life. This was the woman before her life had turned upside. Before despair had caused her to take her life. Jaxx waited as Maddy absorbed what she was looking at. She looked perplexed.

"What's bothering you?" Jaxx asked.

"Don't you think it's weird that she has a portrait here?" Maddy asked. "After all, she had a reputation, and she wasn't wealthy. Who would have paid to have her portrait painted?"

"An artist she was in love with."

Maddy spun around to see an elderly man standing at the entrance of the room. He was fastidiously dressed in dark gray slacks, perfectly pressed and a soft gray dress shirt. A light purple tie added a touch of panache to his outfit. A plastic name tag identified him as Robert Blenning.

"But I thought she was in love with Cooper Grey."

"Ah, you know the story. That was later. This portrait was painted when she was around seventeen. The artist was a traveling man. It was a common practice. He arrived in town and displayed his talents. The wealthy would commission him to paint their portraits. Often, they would supply a guest house for him to set up shop and he would stay as long as people would pay to have the portraits made. He spotted Madeline and insisted he paint her. She didn't have any money, and the town people unkindly guessed what services she exchanged for the portrait. She was young and impulsive. She fancied herself in love. He was experienced and skilled in many things. By the time he had left, she had a portrait and a tarnished reputation."

By now the gentleman was standing next to Madeline and Jaxx. He looked at her then glanced up at the portrait.

"The resemblance is astounding," he mused.

"How long after this did she throw herself off the lighthouse?"

"She was nineteen when she died. Rumor had it she had taken up with Cooper Grey. He had no intention of making her his wife. The rest is history, I'm afraid." The man shook his head, disappointed in the decision of the woman from the past. "Do you have any other questions?" Mr. Blenning queried.

"No, not now. Wait, how many more rooms are there to go through?" Maddy asked.

"After this room we suggest you head upstairs to see some period bedrooms. The silk wallcoverings are exquisite. If you want to climb to the third floor, you will be in the ballroom. That room houses more recent history. You will see several ball gowns and photographs from social gatherings and charity functions from that past sixty years or so. It's interesting. Then you can come back down and finish up with a look at the kitchens. The gardens in the back are also open to the public."

Maddy looked at Jaxx, inclining her head to the stairs. He gestured for her to lead the way and climb the stairs. They wandered through several bedrooms, a couple outfitted for women, one nursery and a child's bedroom, and one very masculine bedroom. When they came back to the central stairs, they climbed the next flight and entered a large ballroom with a wooden dance floor and sparkling crystal chandeliers. Mr. Blenning was dusting several display cases. He reminded them if they had any questions, he would be happy to help.

Positioned around the room were mannequins dressed in ballgowns from various time periods, some created by very famous designers. Over and over again the name Grey was displayed prominently on the identifier cards. Bored with the finery, Maddy moved over to the photographs which hung on the walls. Black and white pictures of glittering party goers gave a glimpse of parties long past. Most of the pictures showed well-heeled people posing, often with champagne or out on the golf course. A couple of pictures captured some graceful sailboats in the harbor.

"Maddy look. It's Mirabelle." Jaxx stood in front of a picture which was taken at a Christmas party. Everyone was in a festive mood and Mirabelle Grey was featured in the center wearing a stunning ballgown with a full-length fur coat tossed casually over her shoulders. Her hand rested in the crook of the elbow of a handsome young man. Maddy read the card. *Mirabelle and Drummond Rentz arrive at the Snow Ball in style.*

Rentz.

Maddy's mother's maiden name.

Giselle Rentz.

"Jaxx!"

He looked at her pale face as she swayed. He caught her in his arms, pulling her tight into his chest.

"Maddy, honey. What is it?" He stroked her long hair as he murmured against the top of her head his lips brushing against her. He studied the picture.

Mr. Blenning hurried toward the couple, concern showing in his face.

"Is something wrong? Is the young lady okay?" A glass of water perhaps?" He wrung his hands unsure of how to proceed.

"A glass of water, please," Jaxx said, the command in his voice not to be ignored. Mr. Blenning looked surprised at first and then snapped into action, hurrying away on his mission.

"Maddy. Look at me." Again, it wasn't a request, but a command.

Her tear stained face turned toward his. Her eyes filled with the look of utter defeat. Before Jaxx had a chance to question her again, Mr. Blenning came hurrying back. Jaxx took the glass of water from him and handed it to Maddy, who took it with trembling hands.

"Drink it," Jaxx said, his voice softening as he watched her shake. "Mr. Blenning, what can you tell me about this picture?" Again, the voice of a man who expected to be obeyed.

"Why that's Mirabelle Grey and Drummond Rentz. Well, at the time it was Mirabelle Rentz. They were married. She was a lovely lady, the belle of the town. Everyone loved her and they were the happiest couple. She was one of the prominent Grey's, of course. He came from a nice family, but they were far from well to do. Ms. Grey didn't care. Her family wasn't happy, of course, but Mirabelle loved him. She always said it didn't matter where you came from or how much money you had, but what you were made of and how you treated people is what mattered. I fear she may have misjudged the man."

"Why is that?" Jaxx asked, his arm tight around Maddy.

"Why, he left her, of course. When she needed him the most, he walked away, the poor thing."

"He left her because she couldn't produce a child?" Maddy said, her eyes bright with unshed tears. "What happened to him?"

"There was a very messy divorce, causing Ms. Grey profound public embarrassment. She was already suffering depression from the loss of her babies. She let her attorneys handle the divorce and she disappeared behind the doors of that big Victorian house she lives in. Drummond Rentz remarried and had a child, I believe. I do remember he made some poor business choices and lost whatever money he had received from Ms. Grey. He became a drunk, and I believe became ill and died. My guess is cirrhosis of the liver."

"Do you know, or can you find out the name of his child?" Maddy asked.

"Of course." Mr. Blenning nodded. "I'll be right back."

"Maddy, honey. What are you thinking?" Jaxx asked her, watching her carefully. She was so pale and seemed so small

"I think I know my connection with Mirabelle."

"But you already knew that. Cooper Grey. Right?"

"No. Closer than that." Her voice trembled and she struggled to maintain control.

Mr. Blenning returned holding a piece of paper.

"I found some information. Drummond Rentz had a daughter. Her name was Giselle."

"My mother," Maddy whispered.

"Your mother?" Mr. Blenning echoed. "Isn't that interesting. I thought, with the resemblance to Madeline Abuchon, you might be descended from her line."

"I am," Maddy said miserably.

"So, you're telling me that you are the granddaughter of Mirabelle's ex-husband?" Jaxx said, thinking of the ramifications.

"Which makes her interest in me even more disturbing," Maddy said, angry now, moving past the shock and sadness and throttling in to full on pissed. "Thank you for everything, Mr. Blenning. You have shed some light on a lot of questions I've had for some time." She reached out to shake his hand. The elderly man took her hand in his.

"It's my pleasure to help, but I'm afraid it just caused you pain. Miss... I never got your name."

"Maddy. Maddy Grey. My name is Maddy Grey."

18

*M*addy strode out of the historical society, fuming. The gears in her head were turning a mile a minute and Jaxx was surprised that he had to hurry to keep up with her. She was making a beeline for the beach. He knew she was hurt and angry, and that made him angry, but he had to admit, he loved the fire in that girl. She was a force to be reckoned with, and he liked that a whole lot more than the girl who looked like she had been kicked. She was up and ready for a fight.

"So where are we headed?" he asked, matching her stride.

"I'm going to see Miss Mirabelle Grey," she spat, her words clipped.

Jaxx had to hide his smile. She was positively beautiful when she was angry. Her eyes were flashing just like the portrait of Madeline Abuchon, and she looked dangerous.

"Would you like me to go with you? I can have your back."

"That's entirely up to you," she said, hardly thinking about what was coming out of her mouth.

"Well, I guess that is true of just about everything, but if you would like backup, I'm here for you," he drawled. "We can go together now while you are all riled up, or we can stop and regroup, maybe have a bite to eat to go with that milkshake we had earlier. Then you can think about what you want to say. Maybe make a plan."

"I thought a surprise attack would be right up your alley," she said, looking at him sideways.

"Yep, it is, but it is supposed to be a surprise to the enemy, not a surprise to the attacker, too." He gave her a lopsided grin that she couldn't help but return.

She stopped in her tracks and turned to him.

"Jaxx, I'm confused and hurt and pissed. I feel like I don't know who I am anymore, and I just don't know what to do. I want to confront her. I want to know why she interfered in my life, and I question her motives."

"I get that. I do, too, but it's better to be prepared. You need to be strong and ready in case she tries to knock you off your feet."

He reached for her hands, folding them together in his. He pulled her in to him and kissed her on the lips. At first her lips were tense, resisting, then they yielded. All of the sudden he didn't care that they were in full view of the public. He wanted to claim her, protect her, conquer her enemies. He kissed her deeper, parting her lips and exploring her mouth. She responded with an urgency that surprised her.

"Get a room!" A car horn honked, and a leering teenager laughed as he sped by them. Jaxx took Maddy's hand and led her down the street, turning on the street that held his new home. Silently, he unlocked the door and led her in.

Betty greeted them with a wagging tail, happy to see them. Jaxx led the dog back out to the porch and closed her in.

"Sorry girl," he said. "You have to wait this one out."

He led Maddy to the bedroom, kissing her as he brought her to the bed. Mabel had assured him that the cottage was supplied with fresh linens. He reminded himself to thank her for that when he sent her his next rent check.

At the last minute, he stopped and looked at Maddy, pulling her gaze into his eyes.

"Is this okay?" he asked her. "Are you ready for me to make love to you?"

She nodded, her eyes huge and luminous.

"Say it," he commanded her.

"Make love to me," she whispered. "Please."

* * *

axx stared at the ceiling as Maddy slept soundly on his shoulder. His mind was working. He wouldn't interfere. This was her fight, but he needed to make sure he had considered all outcomes. His little spitfire had calmed down some. She had turned her anger and pain on him and had made love fiercely, and he had let her, but when she was ready, he was going to do it again. This time it would be sweet and slow. Just the thought of it made him moan.

"What?" Maddy lifted her head and looked at him steadily.

He moved on top of her and kissed her eyelids. She mewed like a kitten.

He liked that. He moved down to her throat and then her breasts, giving every cell of her body the attention that it craved. He had a feeling she hadn't been treated this way, worshipped like she was the most important thing in the moment. Each time she reached for him, to pull him down on top of her, he made her wait, making her tremble with anticipation. This was going to take some time, and when she finally could stand it no longer, he took her to a place she had never been before.

19

*J*axx led Maddy to a booth in the corner, smiling as he remembered they had first met at the Mizzen Mast. She was exhausted but calm and feeling more settled than she had in a long time.

Izzy came over with a couple of menus. She was going to ask what they wanted to drink, but she stopped herself and looked at the couple. Things had shifted between the two of them.

"How are you doing, Maddy?" Izzy asked with a sly smile.

Maddy blushed and Jaxx slid closer to her in the booth, putting a protective arm around her. He didn't know Izzy well. Her appearance; the piercings and the tough exterior, made him even more protective of Maddy, but when his eyes slid up to meet Izzy's he saw wisdom there. She nodded at him slightly. His posture backed down but was still on alert, letting Izzy know that he was okay with her for now, but she'd better not come on too strong with Maddy.

Izzy almost laughed at him and told him to lighten up, but when she looked closer at Maddy, she saw traces of a haunted look shadowing her eyes. Something bad was up.

"Scoot over, lady," Izzy demanded sliding into the booth with them. "What's going on and don't tell me nothing. That won't fly, and

I don't have time for games." She gestured for the waitress to bring them three beers and she settled against the back of the booth waiting Maddy out.

"Izzy, what do you know about Mirabelle Grey?"

Izzy's eyes narrowed. This was a turn of events.

"Why do you ask?"

"Because this woman has apparently meddled in my life since the day I was born, and I want to know what the hell business I am of hers. I was going to ask her today, but Jaxx distracted me." Maddy smiled wanly.

Izzy slid her eyes to Jaxx, communicating her thanks. He just smiled and nodded. Jaxx recognized a kindred spirit. Izzy was a protector.

"First of all," Izzy began, "Mirabelle Grey is often misunderstood."

Maddy snorted, then waited quietly as the waitress placed the beers on the table.

"Right," Maddy said, the disgust showing in her voice.

"Were you guys planning on getting something to eat?" Izzy asked. "We can get that going, and then we can talk. What would you like?"

"What do you suggest?" Jaxx asked, his stomach growling loudly. It broke the tension as Maddy giggled and Izzy grinned.

"I would suggest the Buffalo chicken sandwich on garlic bread with a side order of sweet potato fries and a chef's salad."

"That sounds perfect," Maddy said and Jaxx nodded in agreement.

"Let's make it three, and I'll join you. If that's okay?" Izzy leveled a look at Jaxx.

"The more the merrier," he replied. He was enjoying the sparring.

"Izzy will best you, I guarantee it," Maddy said, as Izzy went to put the order in.

"I doubt it, although my guess is, she is a worthy opponent, especially where her friends are concerned."

Izzy came back and slid next to Maddy. She picked up Maddy's hand and held it between the two of her own. She was surprised how cold Maddy's hand was.

"Maddy, you know as well as I do that people aren't one dimensional. You aren't, I'm not, and I'm suspecting Jaxx here isn't. That's what makes us special and unique. Mirabelle is no different, except she is an old lady who is set in her ways. But honey, her life has sucked."

"I know all about her life sucking. I'm sorry for that, I really am, but it has nothing to do with me."

"You're right. You have nothing to do with it, and neither does anyone else for that matter, but despite the fact that her life has been full of misery, she has made it a priority to make sure other people's lives don't suck."

"What are you talking about?"

Izzy took a deep breath and chose her words carefully.

"Mirabelle has been the financial backer for many people in Grey's Harbor, and they are completely unaware of it. She's helped a lot of your friends. Maeve, for one. Mirabelle was a stakeholder in the building that houses the Cathead Diner. Mirabelle took a loss on it so Maeve could afford it. Maeve had no idea, and neither did anyone else. And the only reason I'm privy to this was because she helped me. I didn't trust her. I wouldn't trust her, so she showed me her cards, so to speak with the promise that I would never tell Maeve. I expect you to honor that promise I made."

"Of course," Maddy said, and Izzy knew that she wouldn't breathe a word of it. Izzy looked at Jaxx and knew he was to be trusted, too.

"Over the years, I've noticed that when things were going south for people something would come along to change their luck. Much of the time, I suspect it was Mirabelle. I wouldn't doubt that it has happened for you, too." Izzy looked at Maddy, waiting for a reaction. She didn't get one because the food arrived at that moment. Izzy thought that maybe it was the way it was supposed to go.

"Good call," said Jaxx after he bit into his sandwich. "This is fantastic,"

Maddy nodded in agreement as she bit into hers. She didn't realize how hungry she was until that first bite, and it was everything she could do not to bolt it down. When she glanced at Jaxx, she realized his sandwich was already gone. He was feeling the same way. She started to giggle furiously thinking about the way they had worked up a hunger. Jaxx and Izzy looked at her like she had lost her mind.

"Stress is getting to her," Jaxx said mildly.

"Obviously." Izzy popped a fry into her mouth and chewed it. "Maddy, when you do decide to talk with Mirabelle, please keep in mind that there is more than one way to see something. Each side is different and not necessarily better than the other. It's a hard thing to learn, but I think it applies to all things Mirabelle. Now I have a bar to tend to. You two enjoy your evening and take care of each other. I think both of you need someone you can count on." She held Jaxx's eyes and smiled into them. "And I think you both may have found that someone." She picked up the empty plates and made her way back to the bar.

"That's the thing about Iz," Maddy said. "She has no trouble speaking her mind."

"I like that about her," Jaxx admitted.

*M*addy and Jaxx walked hand in hand back to Maddy's cottage where they collected Jaxx's truck so he could move his belongings into his new rental. They stopped at the hotel where Jaxx gathered his things and Betty's food, bed, and dishes. Then they loaded the truck and drove to Jaxx's cottage.

Maddy walked Betty so she could do her business while Jaxx set up the cottage to suit him. When she brought Betty back in, the dog nosed around until she found her bed next to the living room fireplace. There she turned around three times and plopped down on her cushion facing the couch where Jaxx and Maddy were sitting. She kept her eyes opened, watching her master. For the first time ever, Jaxx's vibe wasn't thrumming. He was quiet and calm. Betty watched for a minute more, then closed her eyes with a sigh. In minutes she was snoring softly, content in her new home.

"So," Jaxx said as he played with the ends of Maddy's hair where it tumbled over her shoulders and down her arms. "What are you going to do next?"

"I think I'm going to work on the window tomorrow morning. Then I'll see if Mirabelle is available. If so, I'm going to call on her. I think it's time Mirabelle and I have a heart to heart conversation."

"Do you want me with you?" Jaxx asked, not looking at her so as not to pressure her.

"I don't know. I need to think about that."

"That's fine. You've got time to make up your mind. You've got all the time in the world."

20

*M*addy looked over the window assessing the damage. This one didn't have the amount that the first window did. The repair on this one would go quickly. She made patterns of the pieces that needed replaced and cleaned the broken glass from the came. She cut the replacement pieces quickly, her fingers flying, her mind working.

Jaxx knocked on the Dutch door when she was finishing up her final cuts. He grinned at her and stepped into the studio. Her face was freshly scrubbed, and her hair was pulled back in the familiar ponytail, wisps escaping from the elastic, framing her face. He wanted to brush those pieces away from her forehead and plant kisses there. *Damn*, he had it bad.

"Hey," she said.

"Hey."

Jaxx crossed the studio and pulled her into his arms, kissing her. *This is nuts,* he thought. *I just dropped her off a couple of hours ago, but I can't get enough of her.*

"Mmm. You smell great," he told her as he buried his head in her hair.

"It's amazing what a shower will do. You don't smell so bad your-self," she teased.

"Are you ready to see Mirabelle?"

"Yes. I am."

"What brings you out here on a Sunday, Madeline?" Miss Mirabelle said as she ushered Maddy and Jaxx into the house.

"It's Maddy. My name is Maddy."

"I'm sorry. Maddy. Is there a problem with my windows?"

"No. The windows are going very well, actually. I wanted to talk with you about Drummond Rentz and your naming rights."

"I see," said Miss Mirabelle as she paled slightly.

Score one for Maddy, Jaxx thought as he watched Mirabelle's reaction. She wasn't expecting this. She was expecting Maddy to keep her head buried in the sand. Jaxx smiled. He was proud of Maddy. She looked calm and confident.

Mirabelle considered Maddy for a minute trying to gauge how this exchange was going to go.

"Please come into the kitchen. I was about to have brunch. Will you join me?" She gathered her dignity and regained her composure and led them to the back of the house into a large kitchen with a huge central table. By that time, Mirabelle was again in complete control.

"Mary," Mirabelle called. "I have guests. Please accommodate them."

"Tea or coffee," the late middle-aged woman at the stove asked as she turned around to see who she was going to accommodate.

"Whatever you have ready, thank you," said Maddy.

"I have both, and plenty of it. Miss Mirabelle prefers tea, but Henry needs a pot of coffee on all day, so it's always ready."

"Henry?" echoed Maddy, her mind swirling with the possibilities. Mary turned to hide her smile and Miss Mirabelle threw back her head and laughed loudly. The unaccustomed tones from her throat sounded rusty.

"Maddy, dear. Henry is the gardener, and my driver, and whatever else I need done. I am past the age to care about peccadilloes."

It was Maddy's turn to blush, but inwardly she breathed a sigh of relief. The ice was broken. Miss Mirabelle gestured to the chairs at the large central table inviting Jaxx and Maddy to have a seat.

"I don't want to intrude on your meal, Miss Mirabelle. I can come back at a better time," Maddy said, her good manners outshining her need for answers.

"You're not intruding. Mary always makes large portions for brunch. She knows I can nibble on bacon all day long." Mirabelle smiled and sent a conspiratorial glance at Mary, who waved a spatula at her and finished spooning creamy scrambled eggs into a large bowl. She set it on the table with a stack of buttered toast and a large platter of bacon. Even Jaxx couldn't hide his surprise at the amount of meat on the plate.

"Henry and Mary will be joining us," Mirabelle said simply as she poured a cup of tea from the pot Mary placed in front of her. Maddy and Jaxx helped themselves to coffee and within minutes a robust elderly man clomped into the kitchen, glancing at Maddy and Jaxx and made his way to the sink to wash his hands. In minutes the odd assortment was seated at the table.

Miss Mirabelle cleared her throat then led the group in grace. Maddy was surprised and wondered if it was a regular event or something meant to throw her off guard. When she peeked, she discovered that both Mary and Henry looked like two devoted church goers deep in prayer. When Mirabelle was finished, she passed the bowl of eggs to Maddy and invited her to help herself.

"Dig in," Mirabelle declared, almost giddy with excitement. Her cheeks were rosy pink and her eyes were shining. Maddy suddenly realized that Mirabelle looked actually happy. She also realized that this must have been something Mirabelle had always wished for, to share the table with the girl she wanted for her own. Maddy's heart squeezed inside her chest. *This elderly woman only wanted to love her.*

Maddy shook her head. *Mirabelle wanted to possess her. She tried to buy her. She mustn't go all soft now.* Jaxx squeezed her thigh under the table. He was fully aware of the internal struggle she was having, and he wanted her to know he was there, that he had her back.

Mirabelle introduced everyone and led the small talk engaging Henry with a discussion of the garden's progress. He was happy to tell her all about the state of the perennials and which annuals were suffering from the lack of rain. It was all so normal except for the bizarre surroundings and the rich Grande Dame sharing a kitchen table with the help.

Henry finished up, excused himself, and planted a kiss on the top of Mary's head, thanking her for another wonderful meal. She shooed him out the door. After making sure everyone had their fill, Mary began to clear the table. Maddy jumped up to help her. Again, Mary shooed her away.

"I'm sure you came here to talk with Mirabelle. I have this, but thank you for the offer," Mary said with a smile. "You were always a good girl."

"You knew me as a child?" Maddy said.

"Of course, I did. Mirabelle take this child and her man into the sitting room and straighten this all out. It has gone on long enough." With that Mary turned her back, her hands loaded with dishes and made her way to the sink. Mirabelle rose from the table, a tiny glimmer of fear in her eyes. The showdown was inevitable.

"I don't want it sugar-coated. I want the truth...all of it," Maddy stated refusing to sit. She wanted to stand her feet planted firmly facing Mirabelle. Maddy refused to acknowledge how frail, old, and small the woman looked. She had shrunk before Maddy's eyes. The joy she exuded at lunch was just a memory now.

"You need to sit, please Maddy. You're making this difficult."

"Difficult?" Maddy said, shocked at how angry that statement made her. "It's difficult for you? I'm sorry." Her voice was dripping with sarcasm.

Mirabelle's eyes slid over to Jaxx. He was watching Maddy, afraid she was just on the edge of losing control. *Easy,* he thought, sending her the message with his eyes. Mirabelle didn't miss the look or the meaning, or the light in his eyes when he looked at her.

"Maddy," Jaxx said softly. "Come sit next to me. Let's give Miss Mirabelle a moment to collect herself." The power shifted firmly to Maddy, giving her the choice to be benevolent. She took it.

Once Maddy was settled, Mirabelle took a deep breath.

"You know all about your link to Madeline Abuchon and Cooper Grey."

"I do. You can skip that part. Let's move on to where your ex-husband is my grandfather and how you tried to buy me," Maddy said coldly.

"Drummond Rentz was a coward," Mirabelle stated calmly. "He didn't have the backbone to stand next to me and weather the storm, nor did he have the courage to be a good businessman, or a good husband and father to his daughter. He died a drunk and a waste."

"What happened to his wife and daughter?"

"They stayed in Grey's Harbor. His daughter Giselle went to college and came back a little on the wild side. She, like her father, struggled with alcoholism, but seemed to get it under control. She fell in love with your father and they made a life together. I think you figured out that Giselle was your mother. Your grandmother, Helen Rentz passed away from pneumonia, shortly before you were conceived. That put your mother in a downward spiral. She started drinking again. That's when I stepped in. I told your father my connection to his wife and offered to help her. I was able to get her into one of the finest rehab facilities on the east coast. When she came back, she was more settled and focused. She started producing art again, and your father dabbled with her. Then Giselle became pregnant. Once again, she started to doubt her ability to cope. She was afraid they wouldn't be able to afford a child, that she wouldn't be a good mother.

I told her I would help, but that there were to be strings attached. I would help them financially as long as she didn't touch alcohol, and I asked that I be allowed to name the child. Giselle agreed."

Jaxx watched Maddy as the story unfolded. Her eyes were bright with tears. He could feel her world shattering, the secrets cutting her like tiny shards of glass.

"What about my father? Didn't he have a say in this?"

"Your father was a realist, and he loved your mother and you more than life itself. Your mother spent money like it was going out of style, and he had trouble making ends meet. My financial help was a blessing for him. We agreed that your mother would have to work, being productive and helping support the family would give her a purpose and a reason to stay sober." Mirabelle's eyes softened as she watched the tears which were now flowing freely down Maddy's cheeks. "When you came, she found a new reason to stay sober. She loved you so much. I think she surprised herself how much she loved you. We had agreed that she would bring you here so I could have you in my life, too. I know I am a selfish old woman. I wanted a child so badly, but it never was to be. Without a child, I couldn't be a grandmother. Then there you were. A Grey. A relative. A child of Cooper Grey like me. I didn't think it would hurt. I didn't think it would matter if you called me Grandmother."

It was Mirabelle's cheeks which were wet with tears now. Maddy looked at the broken woman before her. A woman who had known nothing but grief and pain. A woman who only wished to love a child and be loved in return.

"Was I kind to you?" Maddy whispered. "Did I call you Grandmother?"

"You did," Mirabelle said with a wistful smile. "But it was our undoing. Your mother heard it and went wild. She accused me of trying to steal you from her. She said I tried to buy you from her. I did nothing of the sort. I know the pain of losing a child. I would never ask another woman to go through what I went through. But she didn't understand that, and she took you from me. She ripped you from my arms and never let me hold you again."

Miss Mirabelle's hands trembled with the memory. She closed her eyes in pain, wanting to shut out the world, fearing she had lost Maddy a second time. When she opened them again, she found Maddy on her knees in front of her, arms opened. Mirabelle sat still, afraid to move until Maddy leaned forward and gathered the old woman tight into her embrace.

21

"*T*hat's the last of the windows, Mirabelle," said Maddy as Jaxx and Ryker applied the final piece of moulding.

"They look beautiful, dear. I couldn't be more pleased."

"I'm pretty happy with them myself." She stood in the parlor looking at the windows and at the sun streaming through them. The colored glass cast brilliant shadows on the floor and walls. Impulsively Maddy stepped into a red patch.

Mirabelle clapped her hands in delight.

"You used to do that as a child. You used to hop from colored shadow to colored shadow. You loved those windows."

"I still do. Mirabelle, my childhood here influenced my whole life. I can't help but believe that these windows brought me to the glass artist that I am today. It's crazy the circle we've come."

"I've found something I want to show you. Would you humor me?"

"Of course, Mirabelle. What can I do?"

"You can accompany me to the tower room. It'll take me a while to climb all those steps. Jaxx, would you accompany me, too? Perhaps lend some assistance? Ryker, you can join us. No sense you being down here by your lonesome." She smiled at him, appreciating the friendship he had with her Maddy.

Together they made their way slowly up the multiple flights of stairs. Miss Mirabelle had to rest every few steps, but the young people waited patiently and chatted about town gossip, making certain Mirabelle didn't feel self-conscious.

When they finally made it to the tower room, Mirabelle sank gratefully into the rocking chair that was placed near the east window.

Ryker whistled a low tone.

"Mirabelle, this is incredible." Maddy gasped as she turned around the tower staring at the sweeping vista, the beach, the ocean, and the village of Grey's Harbor. She could see all the way to the estuary and see tiny boats bobbing in the river near Cadigan's Marina.

"Look, dolphins," Jaxx said, watching the pod swim parallel to the shore.

"This is where you used to sit, hoping to catch glimpses of me at the beach, isn't it?"

"Yes, I watched Grey's Landing every day, hoping you would come out and play. You loved to build sandcastles. I just could never see what they looked like, but I imagined the care you took creating the details only to be washed away by the sea. You were such a happy child on the beach. As you got older, you were joined by your friends. Sometimes I would watch the flames from the bonfires at the old lighthouse, and I would imagine you with Ryker, Maeve, and Tank. I was so happy you had found good friends who cared for you."

"You kept an eye on me throughout my whole life, didn't you?"

"I did. I tried not to interfere, but I made sure that you were taken care of, that you had what you needed."

"Like what? What did you do?" Maddy asked.

Mirabelle hesitated.

"No more secrets," Maddy warned.

Mirabelle sighed.

"You remember that scholarship you got, the full ride to college."

"You didn't," Maddy cried out. "I thought I got that on my own merit."

"You did," Mirabelle assured her. "I went to make that happen, but you had already won the scholarship. It's just that there was another child who needed it. I asked that the university award it to her, but use my money to fund your scholarship, a second one. So, you see, I didn't really help you. I helped someone else."

Maddy smiled at the meddling old woman. Her heart was in the right place.

"What is it you wanted to show me?" Maddy asked.

"It's in this old trunk." Mirabelle pointed at a large antique steamer trunk. "It is filled with a few things left from a Grey estate. Maddy, did you ever wonder why the transom above the front door of your cottage looks odd? Too plain."

Maddy thought about it for a minute.

"I hadn't really considered it, but you're right. It's a little odd."

"That's because it's missing something. Ryker, would you mind opening that trunk. Yes, that quilt. Careful, it's holding a piece of glass."

Ryker lifted the long wide package and placed it on the floor. At Mirabelle's direction he unwrapped it.

Maddy began to smile. She was looking at the missing piece from her cottage. It was a stained-glass transom window. Graceful cut pieces of colored glass spelled out the name Grey's Landing. A few pieces were broken, and the entire window was warped, but Maddy knew she had the skills to fix it.

"Take it home with you, repair it, and put it back where it belongs. I assume you're okay now with the cottage having its rightful name, even if that name is Grey?" Mirabelle said, her eyes twinkling.

"Yes, Miss Mirabelle. I have come to grips with my name and my ancestors. I am proud to call myself a Grey." She leaned over and gave the frail old woman a hug, being careful not to hurt her. Mirabelle wrapped her arthritic hands around Maddy's arm, clinging to her, trying to pull a lifetime of hugs out of that moment.

"When I am gone, all this will be yours," Mirabelle said. "I'll be happy to know that you have your rightful home." She stared out the window to the place she watched the young Maddy grow.

"Mirabelle, I don't want your home, your estate. I love my cottage by the sea, and that's all I want."

"Hush, child. This is all yours. The papers have already been drawn up."

Maddy flashed back on that unpleasant afternoon when she met Miss Mirabelle's attorney. She couldn't imagine how that had gone.

"If I remember correctly, your attorney was adamant that I not reap any benefit from my association with you."

"John Lavish? He's an ass. He thought he was going to manage my estate into a subdivision and line his pockets full of cash. I sent him packing. Sometimes I misjudge men. It's a bad habit of mine." She leveled her eyes at Ryker and Jaxx and stared at them until they squirmed. "I hope neither one of you let me or Maddy down. I would be very put out." She said sternly, then laughed with glee. She was a happy old woman, surrounded by young people. Oh, she wished it had just happened earlier. She had such little time left.

EPILOGUE

"So, what are you going to do with the house, Maddy?" Jaxx asked her as they walked away from the open grave. It was a gray day in the little Methodist cemetery on the hill.

"Mirabelle and I talked about it. Just before she died." She slipped her hand into Jaxx's, the engagement ring still feeling new and foreign on her finger. "I told her I wanted to make it a place for artists. I want to turn the rooms into places young artists can come to stay, to paint the ocean or to weave the patterns the waves make on the sand. I could make studio spaces in the basement. There are lots of cool rooms down there, and the carriage house can be set up with kilns for ceramic and glass. There is even an old forge on the property. It'll need work to get it ready for blacksmithing, but it can happen. There are enough funds to make it all happen."

"I think an artist retreat is an amazing idea. If you can't be inspired here, where can you?"

As they reached the car, Jaxx pulled Maddy into his arms. He was so proud of this woman, this woman who had filled a terrible void in his life. This woman who carried the life he had given inside of her.

"Maddy, you are the kindest person I know. You gave Miss Mirabelle the best year of her life. You know that don't you?"

"I just wish it could have happened sooner. I wished I would have always known her."

"If that would have happened, it would have tarnished your relationship with your mother, and Mirabelle never wanted that to happen. She loved you so much, Maddy. Just like I do."

"I love you, too, and I think you're a pretty special person yourself. You protect me and care for me like no other person ever has, and I know you will be an amazing father. I know you will protect our little Belle and keep her safe from harm."

"I promise you that Maddy Grey. I promise to love you and protect you and our children forever. I made that promise to Mirabelle when I asked for her blessing before I proposed to you. I will never let her or you down. I promise. I love you Maddy Grey."

GREY'S HARBOR

Grey's Harbor
A Grey's Harbor Anthology
By
Carol Cassada
Lark Griffing
Piper Malone
Jennifer Sivec
JC Wing

Five Tales of Love and Romance
by the Sea

GREY'S
HARBOR

curated by

THREE QUILLS PRESS

READ THE NEXT BOOK IN THE GREY'S HARBOR SERIES

Continue your visit where you can follow Ryker's story and meet many other characters you'll fall in love with.

Grey's Harbor is a special place where love is born and passions are ignited, where hearts are broken and second chances are plentiful.

Carol Cassada, Lark Griffing, Piper Malone, Jennifer Sivec, and JC Wing have woven together your next favorite story set in this whimsical town with unforgettable characters who fight for love, forgiveness and each other, and discover that second chances are often the best of them all.

Follow the link to purchase

GREY'S HARBOR
A Grey's Harbor Anthology

Then turn the page for a sneak peek at the first chapters of:

HOPE ADRIFT
A Grey's Harbor Story
By Lark Griffing

HOPE ADRIFT

HOPE ADRIFT
A Grey's Harbor Story

By Lark Griffing

A Grey's Harbor Story

HOPE ADRIFT

LARK GRIFFING

CHAPTER 1

*H*ope stepped onto the dock suddenly beginning to question the impulsive decision that landed her here. The last two months were one snap decision after another, some without any thought whatsoever. It wasn't like her. She was always the methodical one, the planner, the one who looked at every aspect before moving forward on anything.

Until two months ago.

When she walked in on Gary.

With his admin.

On his desk.

And it wasn't shorthand she was doing. More like some kind of oral dictation.

Hope shook her head to rid herself of the image that was burned on her brain. The first snap decision was the call to her brother, the attorney. The second was the quick divorce. The third was accepting a job halfway across the country. The fourth, renting a houseboat to live on.

She had lost her mind. Rapidly.

She glanced at the paper in her hand then looked down the wooden dock. It was in the last slip, a small boat, suitable for the river and estuary, but not the sea. Three pontoons and a flat deck with a small cabin situated in the center. A sundeck graced the top of the cabin with deck chairs and a cheerful flag sporting what looked like a hurricane cocktail. Hope grinned at that. A hurricane sounded good about now.

She looked harder at the boat. A curious, dubious expression flitted across her face. Something about the vessel…like it was home-made or something. Was that possible? Do people make boats? How safe would that be?

"What, you don't like her?"

Startled, Hope jumped at the voice. As she turned, her heel caught in the crack between the dock boards and she lost her balance. A strong hand grasped her wrist and averted a disaster.

She tried to gain her composure as she looked into the bluest eyes she had ever seen.

"If you changed your mind and don't want to rent her, you can just tell me. You don't have to jump in the water for a quick getaway." The blue eyes were crinkled at the corners, and the lips on that face were quirked up in a crooked smile.

"No, I, um, sorry. I've just never seen a houseboat that looked quite like that," Hope said with what she hoped sounded like a non-critical voice.

"And what kind of houseboats are you more familiar with?" the blue eyes asked.

"Well, actually," Hope blushed, "I'm not really familiar with any…" Her voice trailed off.

"Okay, let's get you familiar, and I am Bridger, by the way." He held out his hand waiting for her to take it.

She was still mesmerized by the color of those eyes.

He cleared his throat and started to lower his proffered hand.

Hope managed to blush again, then reached for his hand while murmuring an apology.

"Hope, Hope Elliot, um Chandler. Hope Chandler," she said firmly.

"Are you sure, Hope Chandler?" the eyes asked, trying to suppress a smile.

"Positive," Hope answered, attempting to sound a little frosty but only managing squeaky instead.

"First rule of house boating," Bridger started, "heels are not a good plan." He kept hold of her hand and led her safely along the dock and helped her board the boat. Once on the gleaming wooden deck, he gently let go of her and started the grand tour.

The cabin had a porch roof that extended over the front of the boat. Under that roof was a gas grill, a patio table and a rocking chair. A sliding glass patio door led into the cabin. The deck had a narrow walkway on each side of the cabin leading to the stern. Here there were two more chairs, a steel-banded cooler and several fishing rod holders attached to the railing. A metal spiral staircase led to the top sun deck.

There was another sliding patio door off to the side of the spiral staircase that led into the master bedroom. That door was locked.

Bridger led Hope around to the fore deck again and slid open the patio door. Hope gasped in surprise. They stepped into a beautiful open floor plan. A dinette was in the corner with a L-shaped bench seat, complete with storage in the benches. The living area had a deep, comfortable reclining love seat with a sea chest as a coffee table, and more cleverly hidden storage. A tiny wood burning stove sat in the corner.

A cheerful well-appointed galley was adjacent to the dinette. It was small, but cleverly designed to have maximum counter space and cubbies for kitchen appliances and cookware.

A small hall led out of the living area to a compact but comfortable head with a shower and the bedroom lay beyond. The beautiful space was bathed in light from the patio doors and ingeniously placed high port hole windows that lined the wall just below the ceiling. Golden knotty pine bead board graced the walls, polished to a soft glow.

Hope turned to Bridger, her eyes shining, her hands clasped in front of her with pure joy. She had found a home. She knew it. She could feel it in her bones. This little boat was the start of her new journey. She would start a new teaching job on Monday, and the sale of the home she and Gary had shared would close on Tuesday. One door opening, another closing with a hard slam.

"You'll be okay here," Bridger said softly. He watched her subconsciously rubbing the white line around her finger where a ring had resided for years.

Hope signed the paperwork at the galley counter and Bridger handed her the keys. She hugged herself smiling, thinking she had just made an amazing decision, one that she never would have made in her former existence.

"Do you have things to move in? Can I help you with any bags?" Bridger raised his eyebrows in a question, watching this woman take in the world that was once his most precious place; the first boat he built with his dad.

"Actually, I only have three suitcases and a backpack. Which is a good thing, I suppose," she said, as she looked around at the small space she was going to have to get used to. "Everything should fit in the closets and those built in drawers," she gestured to the storage drawers she could see down the hall in the bedroom, "but I don't know what I am going to do with the empty suitcases." A perplexed look settled on her face as she tried to puzzle out a solution.

Bridger was surprised to find himself attracted to the scrunched-up nose and furrowed brow that came with Hope's solution searching. He wanted to reach out a finger and stroke her forehead, smoothing the thought wrinkles.

It was getting warm in the cabin.

He was starting to think of reaching out a finger to stroke some other parts of her body that he was certain weren't wrinkled, that looked, in fact firm and taut, like that flat abdomen of hers right where it transitioned into a hip bone, right where that sundress draped just so...*Shit.*

"The suitcases are no problem. I have some storage lockers over in the boat building. You can store them there. Let me help you get your stuff on the boat."

"You really don't have to do that," she told him. "But thanks for letting me store my suitcases. That will really help."

The moved out of the cabin and onto the deck in the afternoon sunshine. Hope stretched her head backward and let the sun warm her face. She purred like a cat, with a very self-satisfied smile on her face.

For a brief moment, Bridger thought of laying her down on the top deck and making her purr even louder, her body naked in the sunlight.

Hope looked at him suddenly, electricity snapping between them. She gave him a little smile and moved to the gangway. She knew what she just did to him, and she liked it.

He knew she knew, and he wasn't sure how he felt about that.

CHAPTER 2

*B*ridger followed Hope to her car and helped her remove her suitcases from the trunk. Realizing it was too much for her to handle on her own, she gratefully accepted his offer to help. She held up one finger to Bridger, asking him to wait a minute as she slipped her feet out of her high heels. Scrounging in the back of her car, she came up with a pair of flip flops. Grinning at Bridger, she slid her feet into the sandals and wiggled her toes, enjoying the freedom.

He stared at Hope's toes, the bright pink nail polish contrasting nicely with the smooth tan on her feet. His eyes traveled up her legs—wait, upgrade that—her truly fantastic legs and let his imagination run wild when his eyes were stopped at the hemline of her short sundress.

When his eyes met hers, she was still smiling, like she had won something.

"What are you smiling at, and why do you look so smug?" Bridger asked Hope, not sure he wanted to hear her answer.

She blushed despite her cocky demeanor.

"I was just thinking," she cleared her throat, all the bravado she had a minute ago slipping away. "Never mind what I was thinking. Let's just say that I am starting a new life in a new town. I have a new job, and I am feeling pretty good about things right now."

"Hmmm," Bridger said, knowing full well that was not what she was thinking but deciding to let it go. "Since you now have a new friend, would you like to go grab a bite to eat at a diner that is new to you?" He picked up her suitcases, leaving the backpack for her to carry, and started down the dock toward Hope's new home.

"Maybe. Is the food good?"

"If you like homestyle."

"Is the company nice?"

"If you like casual and relaxed."

"Then I will take that friend up on the offer. When do I meet him?"

Bridger turned to set her straight, but when he saw the teasing smile turning up the edges of that very kissable mouth, he turned around quickly, just in case his trousers gave him away.

He carried the luggage into the bedroom and placed the suitcases on the mattress. Hope stared at the mattress, a realization dawning on her.

"What's wrong?" Bridger asked, looking around in case he missed something when he cleaned the place before her appointment.

"I just realized. When I left, I left everything. I packed my bags with my favorite clothes, but I left everything else. I have to find a store if I want sheets, and towels, and kitchen supplies..." Her voice trailed off.

Bridger figured there was a story there, but it was the wrong time and place.

"The kitchen probably has everything you need, so that shouldn't be a problem. There's a mall out by the freeway, so you should be able to pick some stuff up there. I can take you there before we go eat, or after. Or I can meet you, whatever you want."

"I don't want to impose, and I would like to find my way around. What time did you want to eat? Are you starving now?"

"I'm easy," Bridger said, "Is an hour enough time?"

"Female here. No way I can shop in an hour. Can you give me two? Will you starve before then?"

"No, I'll live. He drew a quick map to the mall for Hope and then left her to settle in and get what she needed. Two hours would give him enough time to take a quick shower and check in on his mom.

When he left the boat, Hope was looking through the kitchen cupboards and making a list. She was humming happily and looked content and at home on his boat. He liked the fact that she was on his boat.

*O*nce her list was made, Hope left the boat, carefully locking the front sliding door. She checked it to be sure she did it right. She laughed at herself. What was she worried about? She had absolutely nothing to steal. She hopped into her car and studied the map. She recognized that she was going to be heading back the way she had come, so she was confident that she would find her way to the mall without any mishap. She thought for a minute, trying to remember if she saw any evidence of a shopping plaza, but she didn't remember anything like that. No worries, she was confident she would find it. As she pulled out of the parking area and drove down the gravel lane, she passed a large blue steel building surrounded by boats on cradles and trailers. In the doorway, Bridger was talking of the phone. He raised his hand in a lazy wave as she drove by. She smiled and waved back. Maybe things really were going to be okay. She was determined to not look back, only forward, and the man waving to her right now was not a bad thing to be looking forward to. *Dinner that is,* she reminded herself. *You're just having dinner.* She shook her head. She was never one to be forward, but damn, maybe she needed to look at herself and perhaps try to be a little less reticent.

*B*ridger watched Hope leave as he listened to his newest customer drone on and on about what he might want on his boat. They had already been through this, but the man needed a weekly update and constant assurance that the boat would be to his exact specifications. Bridger had to continue to remind him that it was too late to change anything but the cosmetic details, as the hull was already formed, and Bridger was beginning to apply the planking. Sometimes he wondered why he got into this business in the first place, but as he walked back into the building and he caught sight of the boat lit by the sunlight, he remembered why. *Wooden boats are beautiful*, he thought. *They have graceful curves like a woman.* His mind flashed to Hope and her curves. *Yep, women and boats have a lot in common.*

Once he managed to get the man off the phone he hopped into his truck and headed out the drive on the way to the home where he grew up. His mom lived alone in a rambling house south of town and he checked on her daily. He glanced at his watch. Now he only had an hour and a half to visit with his mom, get back to his boat, and get a shower before he met Hope for dinner. As long as Mom didn't create a chore for him, he would have plenty of time.

CHAPTER 3

*H*ope unloaded her shopping bags on the small galley counter. She smiled at the blue and white nautical towels she bought for her bathroom. *Cheesy*, she thought, but she couldn't help herself. *Why not?* In her past life, Gary was all about sleek and modern. Appearances were everything. Well, maybe she was rebelling, but she loved the stupid towels.

The sheets made her happy, too. They were also navy and white, but they were a field of forget-me-nots on a white background. Clean, crisp, and feminine. She tore open the package and realized she didn't know where she was going to do her laundry.

The boat didn't have a washer and a dryer.

Well that was dumb of her. She was so enamored with the idea of living on the boat, she had overlooked that little convenience. She wondered what else she overlooked. She looked around her and was instantly charmed again by the boat. *What if she slept on unwashed sheets? Would it kill her?* She rubbed them against her face. They were soft, but still…

Hope heard footsteps on the dock and Bridger's voice.

"Permission to board?"

Hope giggled and opened the sliding screen door.

"By all means. Welcome to your boat, but my new home."

He stepped inside and looked at her. She was still holding the top sheet against her.

"Planning on going to a toga party?" he asked, his eyes sparkling.

"Sure, why not?" she teased back.

He liked that about her. She could laugh at herself.

She was refreshing.

"Seriously, it just dawned on me that my floating apartment doesn't have laundry facilities." She pouted a little.

Bridger cleared his throat. *Damn she was cute.*

"There are laundry facilities in the white marina building. You haven't seen it, yet?"

"No, but it looks like I need to find it." She gestured to the pile of new towels on the counter."

"Well, gather your stuff and you can throw it in the washer before we leave. No one will bother it."

"Are you sure?" Hope looked at him, not trusting that she could just walk away from her things.

"Positive. There are only three of us living at the marina, you, me, and Old Clarence. I'm not doing laundry tonight, and I've never seen Old Clarence do laundry. I suspect he coerces his lady friends to help him in that department."

"Lady friends?" Hope raised her eyebrows.

"Wait until you meet him. He'll probably try to ask you out or invite you over for drinks and a toss in the sheets."

Hope burst out laughing.

"A toss in the sheets? A guy named Old Clarence? You're kidding, right?"

"Not at all," Bridger said solemnly. "Swear."

"Hmmm, does he have money?" Hope asked, a glint in her eye.

"So, you have a price, huh?" Bridger's eye's darkened and Hope felt a flush rise to her cheeks. It wasn't the only part of her body getting warm.

"More than you could afford, I suspect," she teased.

"Did you remember to buy laundry detergent," he whispered in a menacing voice.

Damn it.

He was quick to register her reaction.

"Well, sweetheart," he started in a terrible Bogart impression, "what's it worth to you?"

He leered at her, wagging his eyebrows, trying hard to look sinister.

"For a cup of laundry detergent, I'll buy you a drink. After all, these are clean sheets, not dirty underwear. Not worth much more than a beer."

She stared him down, her hands on her hips in mock anger, the sheet still draped across her body in an odd garden toga motif.

"Okay, I'll take the beer. Are you ready?"

Hope stuffed the towels and the sheets in a shopping bag and followed Bridger out of the cabin, carefully locking the door behind her. She tested it.

Bridger watched how careful she was about making sure the boat was locked.

"Things are pretty quiet and safe here. It's a small town, and people respect other people's property."

"It's a habit. In the city, someone would steal everything out of your car before you could get it locked behind you." She smiled apologetically.

"Not a bad idea to keep things locked, but I didn't want you to worry. You're safe here."

"Thanks, now where is that cup of soap?"

"That's my boat in the first slip. We'll stop there first then I'll take you to the marina building. Can I carry that for you?" He reached to take the bag from her.

"No, I've got it okay, but thanks." She smiled at him making sure he knew she wasn't militant about denying his offer. "If it was heavy, you can bet I would have you carry it."

They stopped at the first slip and Hope stared up at the huge sailboat.

Her mouth dropped open. It was a beautiful wooden boat with graceful curves and brass portholes. Bridger took her hand to help her onto the deck. It required her to climb several steps. Once on deck, it took Bridger a second to drop her hand. She noticed but chose not to say anything.

Bridger's boat was stunning. Easily twice the size of hers, maybe more, it gleamed in the sun, the brass and teak deck highly polished. The mast rose high above her, and she got dizzy looking up as the boat moved gently underneath her. Bridger reached out to steady her.

"I get more movement at this dock than you do, plus a sailboat rides in the water differently. You'll get your sea legs soon."

"Your boat is beautiful," Hope said in a hushed whisper. "You live here?"

"Yep, here or in the houseboat in the next slip."

"Oooh la la…" Hope said, raising her eyebrows. "Two homes next to each other, huh? Pretty impressive!"

"That's also where my office is," Bridger pointed out. "Here, come on below." He shoved the slide-open hatch to the companionway and led Hope down the stairs into the interior of the boat.

They entered a generous salon. There was a small galley to the right of the stairs and a bathroom to the left. A dinette was further in on the right, and a seating area was opposite of the dinette. The fore cabin was where the captain's berth was, and Bridger showed Hope that there were guest accommodations in the aft cabin.

She loved it but felt confined, thinking that her little houseboat was better suited for living. Bridger read her mind.

"The houseboat is more comfortable for staying in the river and hanging out in one place, but this boat can sail the world. I can live in her and travel all I want."

"Have you done that?" Hope asked, curious, but thinking she already knew the answer.

"No." Bridger sighed, "The business hasn't allowed me the luxury." But his face brightened in a smile, "I have taken her to the Virgin Islands and spent some time there, then brought her home." His eyes held a faraway look.

"I bet it was amazing. I've never sailed before," Hope said as she looked at all the electronic equipment wondering what it all did.

"Well, that is going to have to change. I would love to take you on a cruise down the coast." He reached into a cabinet above his head and tossed a laundry pod at Hope. "Here, don't eat it."

She laughed and tossed it in her bag and added the dryer sheet Bridger handed her. Turning, she headed back up the stairs to the deck. Bridger followed and helped her down the steps and back on the dock.

"Aren't you going to close the hatch thingy?" she asked.

"Hatch thingy? No, I'm going to air out the cabin a bit. No one will bother my boat. Let's get this laundry in and get going. I'm getting hungry."

Bridger showed her the marina building complete with laundry and shower rooms in case she didn't want to use the one on the boat. She threw the towels and sheets in the washing machine and added the laundry pod, but only after offering it to the hungry Bridger. He passed.

Satisfied, they made their way to Bridger's truck. As he helped her in, he noticed she didn't have anything in her hands.

"No purse or anything?" he asked, sure they were going to have to go back to her boat.

"Nope, everything I need is in my pocket. I'm good." She smiled at him and he shut the truck door.

Damn, he was beginning to like this woman. She didn't carry a purse. That alone was a big star in his book.

PURCHASE HOPE ADRIFT

From Amazon
or
Click the linked cover below

SIGN UP FOR LARK'S NEWSLETTER

Would you like to know when Lark releases her next book? Do you want a sneak peek at sample chapters? If so, sign up for Lark Griffing's newsletter.

Subscribe now

Or use this URL to subscribe

http://eepurl.com/dH1mzz

ACKNOWLEDGMENTS

Many thanks to my fellow authors and friends who always lend support. A special thanks goes to JC Wing, who is my editor, a fantastic author, and a dear friend. She makes things happen the right way. Also, thank you to Jennifer Sivec, a wonderful author and friend who is always willing to listen and offer advice.

Of course, my dear husband and family are my main champions and supporters. Without them, I am nothing.

ALSO BY LARK GRIFFING

Grey's Harbor Stories

GREY'S HARBOR

A Grey's Harbor Anthology

By Carol Cassada

Lark Griffing

Piper Malone

Jennifer Sivec

J.C. Wing

HOPE ADRIFT

A Grey's Harbor Story

By Lark Griffing

And coming soon

HARBOR TIDES

A Grey's Harbor Story

By Lark Griffing

Gone To the Dogs Camper Romance Series

Teardrops and Flip Flops

Teardrops and Rest Stops

Young Adult:

The Last Time I Checked I Was Still Here

The Starfish Talisman

Short Story Collections

Dog on the Doorstep

ABOUT THE AUTHOR

Lark Griffing is all about stories of adventure and romance. Whether writing about a recent Widowed women discovering life in a teardrop trailer or a teenage girl dealing with evil spirits in her aunt's ancient house on the cliffs above the sea, Lark sets the story in motion and the reader is never really sure where or how it's going to end. Often that reader gets a surprise they weren't expecting, and Lark likes that.

Lark Griffing is a dabbler. Her hobbies are many and varied, from SCUBA diving to backpacking, kayaking to knitting. You never know what you're going to get on any given day if you hang with her.

Her husband and boys are used to her running off in all directions, and they humor her because they know that with Lark, an adventure awaits them. The only members of her family who are not up for the fun are her tabby cat, Dickens and her golden doodle, Maggie. The two of them would prefer staying curled up together holding down the fort until Lark comes bursting back through the door.

Keep up with Lark at her website:

www.LarkGriffing.com

facebook.com/larkgriffing

twitter.com/Lark_Griffing

instagram.com/LarkGriffing

www.ingramcontent.com/pod-product-compliance
Lightning Source LLC
Chambersburg PA
CBHW020909180626
46816CB00007BA/2324